DAYVILLE

BILL HEATON

For Maria, thank you for being my anchor, I love you.

AUGUST 15, 2023

← PROLOGUE

THE SUN WAS SETTING ON CREEKWOOD LAKE, WITH A light breeze shaking the leaves on the surrounding trees. The air was fresh, accompanied by the sounds of birds chirping in the distance.

Gus Collins stood at the edge of his dock that led out to the lake, then looked up at the sky, savoring the beautiful golden glow that illuminated his surroundings. It was a familiar sight he had seen for the last eight years. Not a day went by where he took any of it for granted.

He waited as the sun disappeared behind the trees and the darkness settled, then turned and looked down at the dirt path that led him back to his home and started walking. As he walked, he admired the changing colors of the leaves that hung high above him.

Gus lived alone in his second-story apartment. Many mornings, he would sit at the kitchen table reading the newspaper and having his coffee. During these moments, he would reflect on his life and the events that brought him to where he was.

GUS ENLISTED IN the police academy and spent his entire career with the Dayville Police Department. He began as a rookie police officer, advancing to—and retiring with—the rank of lieutenant. His career included four Unit Citation awards, the Dayville Police Department's Medal for Valor, the Commendation for Community Service, and the Commendation for Exceptional Merit. Even so, all the successes in his professional life couldn't erase the tragedies in his personal life.

It had been eight years since the death of his wife, Janice Collins. They had been high school sweethearts and were married after they both graduated, but during the years since joining the academy, law enforcement had been the central focus of Gus's life.

He would work fifty to sixty hours a week, fully immersing himself in each fresh case, driven by the belief that he could solve them all. This put a strain on their marriage. Gus's career became more of a priority than starting a family with Janice. She would sometimes resent Gus for his choices, but deep down, she still loved him enough that she could never leave him.

HE NOW BELIEVED his career and his life seemed to have come full circle. With success also came a travesty. Gus could never forget the horror of the night of March 29, 1993. The murder of an innocent man in the remote dunes of Southern Dayville. The events left him traumatized for the rest of his life and would always remain in his memory. To dispose of the body and say nothing about it. To dig the grave that would serve as a resting place for Brian Tate.

The years that followed grew more painful. Time did not heal the wounds. Although his work would be a distraction for him, it would also be a daily reminder. Every morning that he would put on his uniform, polish his shoes and his badge, and clean his service revolver, he would think of the past. Over the years, Gus became isolated from everyone, even his own family. He was afraid of letting people see the real man he was.

The truth was now laid out in the letter he held in his hand. Although it wasn't a confession, it conveyed the depth of his pain and the reasons he couldn't bear it any longer. He folded it up and placed it in the drawer of the side table next to his bed, and locked it with a key. His knees cracked from years of arthritis as he walked to the bedroom window. He opened it and threw the key out as far as he could. Following that, he closed the window, proceeded to the kitchen, and poured himself a glass of whiskey. He walked over to the window and admired the view of Creekwood Lake.

It was a lake he had fond memories of fishing with his father years ago. Watching the perfect sunrise view of the lake was his sole source of comfort.

With his drink in hand, Gus wandered around the apartment one last time. He returned to the bedroom and sat on the bed. Glancing at the small framed picture of Janice, he set his drink on the table and picked up the picture. He could feel his eyes starting to tear up.

"I'm so sorry."

Gus put the picture back on the table, his left hand trembling. He was not a man who feared death. In a way, he had been waiting for it to come, a price that he knew he would have to pay someday.

He examined the various bottles of medications behind the picture. They were arranged side by side. He had done enough research to know that would be enough to do the job.

Gus took a handful of pills from each bottle and swallowed them one by one with the whiskey until his palm was empty. He then laid down on the bed and thought for a minute about what he had done, not having a single regret. Gus then took a deep breath, exhaled, then waited.

MARCH 29, 1993

— ONE

TERRY'S FRIENDLY TAP WAS A WELL-KNOWN NEIGH-
borhood bar in the downtown area of Dayville, Rhode Island.
The exterior of the bar was unassuming, with weathered brick
walls and a faded wooden sign hanging above the entrance,
its letters chipped but still legible: *Terry's Friendly Tap–Est.
1948.*

A small neon light was flickering in the window, and the
reflection shone onto the pavement. The inviting ambiance of
the interior radiated a comforting warmth, drawing in residents and tourists.

For thirty-five years, the regulars would come in for drinks
at all hours of the day. They knew that Terry's was a joint for
all, a place to grab a beer after work, meet friends, or just chill
out. The bartender, Joe Duffy, was an old man who could be
rough around the edges, but knew most of the guests by their
first names.

The local workers would come in at the end of their ten-
to-twelve-hour shifts, and others would even come in before
the start of their shifts. The bar itself was a long polished oak
counter, pitted with the dents and nicks of age, but its surface
shone in the dim light fixtures that hung above it. Behind the
bar, there were rows of bottles standing on shelves with the

labels outwards, illuminated by the faint light of the lamps. A jukebox by the side, full of the tracks of Classic Rock and Country, was playing, accompanying the indistinct murmurs of discussion and eruptions of laughter. Terry's would sometimes be the site of trouble with the police; drunken brawls and fights had occurred on more than one occasion. As much as Terry's was known for being rough around the edges, it also was a favorite after-hours drinking spot for off-duty police.

THE WEATHER had been warm on the night of March 29, 1993. The air was heavy with a gentle, almost balmy warmth. A gentle breeze rustled the leaves outside.

It was about seven o'clock that evening, and Terry's was busy with the usual patrons and a few police officers at the end of their shift. Inside, the mood was light, with the low buzz of patrons conversing as usual, mingling around their familiar zones. Sounds of glasses clinking and intermittent laughter mixed with the music from the jukebox.

A few leaves blew in from the street as Claudia Bates walked into the bar. The warmth of the night outside followed her in and stirred the air inside the bar. She would often walk alone to Terry's from her place, which was only a couple of blocks away. A few faces around the bar acknowledged her presence with a nod, and Joe, who knew her well, was pouring her a drink even before she ordered.

Although a life of excessive drinking and a bad smoking habit since her early teens had aged her faster than she wanted, Claudia was still attractive with a thin frame and medium-length brown hair. Twice divorced, she had already led a life full of its share of turbulence.

Claudia made her way towards the bar as Joe set down a Moscow Mule in front of her.

"The usual, I assume?"

"Joe, have I ever told you that you're the best?"

"All the time. Wanna start a tab?"

"I'll let you know after the next drink."

About half an hour later, Brian Tate walked into Terry's alone. He was a muscular young man with long, dirty blonde hair that reached his ears and gave him a handsome and rough look. He looked around at the scenery before him and noticed the empty seat next to Claudia. Brian walked over, sat down at the bar beside her, and waited for Joe to walk over to serve him. Brian looked over at Claudia; attractive, he thought.

Brian was twenty-one years of age and a native of Saratoga, New Hampshire. He was majoring in psychology during his junior year at Chepstow College in Rowe, Vermont, and during an early March college break, he had spent time with friends in Hamden, Connecticut. He was on his way back to resume his studies.

This was the first time Brian visited Dayville, Rhode Island, which he was not even aware existed until a friend suggested an alternate way home that included a shortcut through there to save him a considerable amount of time on the road.

After he sat down, Claudia looked to her left at Brian and felt intrigued by the young man she had never seen before. Brian looked over at Joe again, who didn't seem to notice him, and waited.

"You'll have to flag him down if you want a drink," Claudia said.

"Is the service always this good?" Brian asked with a smirk.

"Only if you're new here. The regulars get preferred treatment."

Claudia then stood up over the bar so she could get Joe's attention.

"Hey Joe, can you spare a second of your time?"

Joe walked over to the end of the bar and gave Brian a quick look over.

"What?"

"Do you have any beer that's made locally?" Brian asked.

"Bentley Ale, if you can handle it. Got an I.D.?"

Brian reached into his inner coat pocket, pulled out his wallet, and placed a New Hampshire driver's license on the bar top. Joe took it and looked at it for a moment, then placed it back on the bar and walked away.

"Pleasant fellow, huh?" Brian asked.

"You'll know quick. He'll either walk back over with a beer or a gun," Claudia said.

To Brian's relief, Joe walked back over with a cold bottle of Bentley Ale.

Brian looked down, reached into his pocket, and took out a five-dollar bill to put on the table.

"Hey Joe, put his on my tab," Claudia said.

Joe nodded as Claudia looked at Brian and smiled. Brian put the money back in his pocket.

"Thanks."

"No worries."

"Next one's on me, then?"

"Fair enough."

"I'm Brian."

"Claudia."

"Nice to meet you."

"Likewise. I don't recall ever seeing you around here before. Are you new to the area?"

"No, just passing through. I was visiting some friends."

"Sounds like fun. Where are you heading from here?"

"Rowe, Vermont."

"Shit, that's a hike for this time of the night. Are you driving straight through after this?"

"I thought about it, but I'm already tired just driving from Connecticut, might just stay at a motel. Are there any around?"

"There's Sherrie's Inn a couple of miles from here. That's the only one that I know of. I heard it's nice, if you don't mind the rats," she said.

"Looks like I'm driving straight through, then."

Brian and Claudia continued to flirt their way through their conversation as the evening went on. After ordering another round of drinks, they became even more friendly.

SEATED IN A BOOTH at the other end of the bar, where the light barely touched him, was Officer Larry Becker, keeping almost invisible. Becker had been with the Dayville Police Department for close to four years, and throughout that period, he had proven to be hardworking and trustworthy. Tonight, he was off duty. He checked in earlier than usual to have a couple of beers with some of the other off-duty officers.

Becker was tall, and his presence was commanding, even in the most casual situation. Despite having cropped dark brown hair that held a bit of gray, suggesting a stressful time with the police force, he maintained a composed posture. He looked as though deep in thought. Hunched over the table, he watched the room with the predatory gaze of a man who did not know the concept of being off duty.

Becker was always popular during get-togethers at Terry's, talking loudly and telling jokes. But underneath it all, Becker was just the opposite. He had taken his work too seriously. During Becker's nearly ten years as a police officer, six with the Garrett, Massachusetts police department and four years with Dayville, he had seen just about everything: from homicides, robberies, rape cases, assaults, and kidnappings; it was the nature of what he had seen that led him to create humorous and funny stories for a sense of relief from his job.

As the night continued at Terry's, the officers sitting with Becker were raucous with laughter. Instead of joining in on the fun, Becker's attentions were focused elsewhere. His eyes were zoned in on Brian and Claudia at the bar as they laughed and continued to drink.

Joe refilled the glass with a drink for Claudia while Brian sat brooding over the beer. His glass was filled to the brim but untouched. Becker watched them with a focused glare. His gaze followed each interaction and each minuscule glance between the two. He studied their every movement, focusing on nothing else around him.

The chattering laugh of the people, the ringing of glasses, and the murmurs from the neighboring tables had no effect on Becker. He bent forward to overhear their conversation but could only hear whispers.

A sudden wave of coldness swept over him as his hand clenched into a fist around the stem of the glass. The officer sitting next to him, Hatfield, could see that he was fighting to keep from squirming uncomfortably. Finally, Becker could not endure it any longer. He slowly stood up from the booth, his gaze fixed on Claudia and Brian with a calm and calculated movement. Then, like a quick flick of a switch, his mood lightened.

"I've gotta horse like a piss race. Order me another one if you bums ain't too cheap," Becker said.

The officers in the booth erupted with drunken laughter and waved Becker away.

"Try not to fall in," Hatfield yelled.

"Wanna come help me out? Doc says I shouldn't lift anything over ten pounds," Becker said.

They all laughed again as Becker made his way out one of the side doors of the bar. Once outside, he rushed to the nearest phone booth.

— TWO

THE PHONE RANG AT SGT. ART KRAMER'S OFFICE around 10:45 p.m. He was putting in yet another late night at the station.

Art Kramer was a veteran police officer with the Dayville police department. His presence was intimidating, just based on his size and look. He was tall and well built, with brushed-back hair with light streaks of gray on the sides and a dark, neatly trimmed mustache. He had an air of confidence about him; he knew his value. It was not cockiness but a vibe that told you that the man was going places. Kramer was a man of ambition, and he acted as if he could take on whatever was ahead.

He wanted to get involved in politics and often served as a consultant for improving administrative operations in the town. Kramer earned the reputation of a man who would get things done. However, depending on the urgency or nature of the goal, he could be ruthless in getting whatever results he was looking for. People close to Kramer also knew he had a hot temper that could get out of control.

Kramer was married and lived in a well-established part of Dayville. The house was as well-groomed as his persona, showing how much he had strived to build a successful image.

Kramer and Chelsea, his wife, had been married for about ten years. Onlookers couldn't help but feel a pang of envy as they watched the couple's blissful display.

Although he could be a loving husband, he also balanced his work life with his hidden life, which included an affair with Claudia Bates.

Kramer had been seeing Claudia for almost a year and kept it hidden from everyone. He never bragged about it to his colleagues, wanting to keep complete secrecy. Although Kramer cared for Claudia, he also could not bring himself to leave his wife for her. He enjoyed being able to live the married life in front of people to boost his public image.

Lately, however, Kramer suspected Claudia was seeing somebody else behind his back. The very idea preyed on his mind, and he could not shake it. Kramer's possessive nature, which was concealed by his formal demeanor, appeared from time to time. He did not like feeling powerlessness, and the possibility of Claudia being close to another man drove him mad.

After following Claudia for several nights at the usual time she would leave for Terry's, Kramer had learned nothing at all about who she was seeing. Each night, after drinking for a few hours, Claudia would leave Terry's, walk one block to her place, check the mail at the door, and then go upstairs alone. After nights of surveillance, Kramer came away with nothing.

Kramer was leaning back in his chair behind his desk, reading a recent case file he was helping with, when he glanced at the phone, checked his watch, and picked it up.

"This is Kramer."

"Art, it's Becker. Is it okay to talk?"

"Yeah, talk to me."

"I'm at Terry's. Got here before Claudia showed up. Art, I think we got him."

Kramer leaned forward in his chair, listening.

"You're sure?"

"It looks pretty legit; he came in not long after her. They've been drinking and chatting for a while now. She's pretty ballsy meeting him here."

Kramer's face was expressionless. He sat in the chair in silence as the moments passed. He took off his reading glasses and rubbed his eyes.

"What do you wanna do, Art?"

Kramer sat for another few moments, thinking things through.

"Well, if he's drinking and he gets behind the wheel, that gives you a reason to have a little chat with him."

"Okay, I'll bring him in."

"No. Take him to the dunes, and I'll meet you there with Collins."

"The Dunes? What's the occasion?"

"Change of scenery."

"Okay, whatever you want."

Kramer then hung up the phone. He leaned back in his chair and stared out the window of his office.

———————

BECKER HUNG UP the phone, came out of the booth, and started walking back to Terry's. He harbored more questions about Kramer's plan. Why the dunes? Why not just take the kid to the precinct? He had seen Kramer lose his temper when receiving unwelcome news in the past, which was something Becker had to experience sometimes. It bothered Becker that Kramer could be so unpredictable.

Becker returned to Terry's, going through the same side door he left out of. As Becker walked back over to the table, he looked over to the end of the bar, where Claudia and Brian were still sitting. Becker walked back over to the booth where the other officers were.

"What happened, old man? Did ya fall asleep on the shitter or something?" one officer asked.

"No, I was banging your wife in the parking lot. She wanted me to tell you to pick up a loaf of bread on your way home," Becker said.

The officers all erupted with laughter once again. As Becker sat back down in the booth, he looked over at the bar. He thought for a moment about what would happen if he just walked over to Brian and told him to get lost now, while he could still breathe. That if he kept talking to Claudia, things would not be in his favor by the end of the night. He could lie to Kramer and tell him that when he got back to the bar, the kid had left. Then again, Becker thought, what if Kramer found out the truth? Would he be in the hot seat and have to face Kramer's wrath instead of Brian? Becker did not want to take that chance.

————

IT WAS JUST after midnight at Terry's. Joe was drying the last of the beer mugs that he just cleaned when he looked at his watch. His favorite part of the night. Joe turned around to face as many of the remaining customers as he could.

"Last Call!"

The officers in the booth with Becker finished the last of their beers, and then they got up to leave. Becker stayed seated in the booth.

"Are you sticking around?" Hatfield asked.

"Na, I'm out in a few. You guys go ahead," Becker said.

The officers then reached into their pockets for money to pay for the bar tab. Becker reached out and grabbed the check on the table.

"Don't bother. I know how much you clowns make, and you can't afford it."

"You sure?" another officer asked.

Becker nodded his head.

"Get outta here before I change my mind."

The officers each went back to the booth, shook Becker's hand, and then walked out of the bar. Becker watched as the remaining customers at Terry's finished their drinks and left. He also watched Claudia and Brian, who were still engaged in conversation.

"Well, Brian, I've gotta say it's been some night. You're quite interesting," Claudia said.

"I wasn't expecting to meet someone like you in a place like this. It was an absolute pleasure spending the evening with you."

"Still thinking about driving to Vermont right now? You won't hit any traffic."

"That depends."

"On?"

"Well, if I decide to get a motel, would you like to hang out for a bit more?"

Claudia looked at him with a little suspicion.

"Well, aren't we being forward?"

"Yeah, I know, I'm sorry. I didn't mean for it to sound like that."

"You're fine, don't worry. I just wouldn't recommend someone like you getting tangled up with someone like me. Go back to Vermont and learn something fun. Next time you decide to come through here, look me up, and we can do this again."

"Deal."

Becker watched as Claudia finished the last of her drink, got up from the bar stool, and picked up her purse. Brian stood up and reached into his pocket, pulled out a wad of bills, counted them, and placed them on the bar top. He then followed Claudia past the bar towards the front door. Claudia waved at Joe.

"Have a good night, Joe."

Joe waved at her without looking up, focusing on counting the cash that was in the register behind the bar.

"Nice meeting you," Brian said.

Joe didn't acknowledge Brian's words. He finished counting the rest of the cash, then walked to the small office behind the bar. He looked over at Becker and stopped for a moment.

"I trust you're not gonna sneak a drink outta here, right?"

"Wouldn't dream of it. Scout's honor!" Becker said as he gave Joe the middle finger.

"Goodnight, Larry," Joe said, shaking his head as he walked through the doorway to the back.

Becker waited a few moments, then got up from the booth. He walked towards the front door and peered out the window into the parking lot. In the distance, he could see Claudia and Brian talking next to what Becker assumed was Brian's car. Becker stood at the door and waited. He watched as Claudia leaned forward and hugged Brian, then she walked to the other side of the parking lot and made her way back toward her place.

Becker continued to watch Claudia until she was far enough out of sight. He then looked at Brian, who was unlocking his car door. Becker waited until Brian got into the car and started it. He then walked out of Terry's and approached the driver's side door of Brian's car.

Becker tapped on the window. Startled, Brian looked out of the window and saw Becker's face. Brian hesitated for a moment, wondering what this stranger was going to do. Dressed in plain clothes, Becker looked like he could be anybody off the street. Brian's body tensed, and his mind went wild, wondering whether this was a sign of a robbery about to happen.

Becker drew out his wallet. He opened it up, and Brian saw a well-shined police badge with a somewhat hidden identity card. The badge made Brian pause. Still skeptical, he lowered the window just enough to listen to Becker.

"Yes, sir?" Brian asked.

"May I please see your driver's license?"

Brian reached into his billfold, pulled out his license, and handed it through the window to Becker.

"I'm going to need you to turn the car off as well."

Brian turned the keys and shut the car off.

"Keys on the dashboard."

Brian did as instructed. He then placed both hands on top of the steering wheel so Becker could see them, and kept his eyes forward. Becker studied Brian's driver's license, not once looking at Brian. After a few silent moments, Brian looked back towards Becker.

"Do you mind if I ask what's going on, what this is all about?"

Becker continued to look at the license.

"Where are you headed tonight?"

"I'm on my way back to Rowe, Vermont."

"For?"

"College. I'm a junior at Chepstow."

"Could've fooled me. You look like more of a Harvard guy."

Brian did not say or do anything. He knew better than to open his mouth and make trouble.

"License says you live in New Hampshire. You say you're going to school in Vermont. The fuck are you doing in Little Rhody? A little out of the way, aren't ya?"

"I was visiting with some friends in Connecticut while on break from school. I took a different way back home that led me through here. Just figured I'd stop off somewhere before the long drive. I was even thinking of getting a room for the night if I got too tired."

"Wow, New Hampshire, Vermont, Connecticut, Rhode Island. You really get around, huh?"

Brian continued to stare at Becker, not knowing what the right response would be. Becker looked back down at Brian's license and studied it again, looking over every detail. He then handed the license back to Brian, who took it and placed it on the passenger seat.

"Were you drinking at all?" Becker asked.

"I had a full beer and half of another," Brian said.

Becker took a few steps back from the car and looked it over, studying the license plates and checking for any broken taillights. He walked back over to the driver's side where Brian was in the same spot, not moving so much as a finger.

"Nice girl you were talking to," Becker said.

"Um, yeah, I guess so."

"She a friend of yours or something?"

Brian stared at Becker, confused by the question.

"No, I just met her tonight."

"Met her tonight, huh?"

"Yes. I'm not lying. We only met a little while ago!"

"Never said that you were lying. No need to get your pecker hard."

Brian was becoming more confused by the conversation, as well as a little annoyed.

"Have I done something wrong?"

"I don't know Brian, have you?"

A few moments passed as Brian sat still in the car, looking

into Becker's eyes. He felt Becker was accusing him of something, although he did not know what.

"Step out of the car, please," Becker said.

"Okay, I'm not sure what I've done, but can you please
tell me what this is all about?"

"Step out of the car, Brian. Don't make me have to ask
you again."

Brian opened the door and stepped out of the car, standing
face-to-face with Becker.

"Turn around and place your hands on the side of the car,
legs apart."

Brian followed the instructions. He stood there as Becker
searched him. After not finding anything, Becker stepped
back. Brian stayed in his position with his hands on the side
of the car. Becker then quickly grabbed Brian's left hand and
put it behind his lower back. He then did the same with his
right hand. Everything happened so quickly that Brian had
no time to react. He then felt the cold metal of the handcuffs
being placed on his hands.

"What the hell!"

"Brian Tate, I'm placing you under arrest for attempting
to operate a vehicle while under the influence of alcohol."

"What, are you kidding me? Please tell me this is some
kind of joke!"

Becker read Brian his Miranda Rights.

"Good God, I've had only two beers, not even that!"

"Get in the back of the car."

"Can I take one of those breathalyzer things? I swear I'm
not drunk or even close to being drunk."

"Get in the car. I'm not gonna ask you again."

Brian looked around the parking lot in confusion. He
assumed Becker was referring to his own car, but Brian's car
was the only one in the parking lot.

"What car?"

"Your car, dickhead."

Becker grabbed Brian and moved him toward the rear passenger door of the car. Becker opened the door and shoved Brian in.

"Don't forget to buckle up," Becker said.

"Look, man, you've got this all wrong. I'm not drunk. Give me some kind of test, and I can prove it. If you don't want me to drive, that's fine. I'll get a room somewhere. You can follow me to make sure. I've done nothing wrong; please, this is some kind of mistake!"

Becker looked down at Brian and glared at him. His eyes said it all. Brian adjusted himself in the back seat and pulled the seatbelt over him.

"This is bullshit," Brian said.

"Keep talking like that, and I'll add obstruction of justice to the list."

Becker shut the door and walked around to the driver's side of the car and got behind the wheel. He took the keys from the dashboard and started the car, then drove out of the parking lot and onto the main road. Becker looked into the rear-view mirror, and his eyes met Brian's.

"Do I need a lawyer or something?" Brian asked.

Becker said nothing and looked ahead at the road.

Brian looked out the passenger window into the wooded darkness. Suddenly, a thought popped into Brian's head. He turned and looked into the rear-view mirror, hoping to look into Becker's eyes again.

"Is this about that girl, Claudia?"

Becker looked into the rear-view mirror, meeting Brian's eyes. They each stared for a moment at each other as if their respective glances answered the question.

"I told you I just met her only a few hours ago. Nothing happened with her."

Becker stared at Brian for a moment longer, and then his eyes focused on the road.

Brian looked away and out the passenger window again. Then he had a moment where he regretted meeting Claudia Bates.

THREE

BRIAN TATE SAT IN THE BACK SEAT HANDCUFFED AND silent, staring out of the window into the darkness. There was nothing he could do to change the situation. He knew without a doubt that he had done nothing wrong. But he also knew there was no trying to convince Becker.

AFTER WHAT FELT like a long, boring drive, Brian sensed the car turning left onto a rough dirt road. The car crept forward, rocking from side to side for a while as they continued driving on the uneven path. He kept looking out the window, trying to see where they were.

"Where the hell are we?"

Becker ignored the question, instead focusing ahead of him. After a few minutes of tense silence, Becker spoke.

"Ever hear of Llangollen Sand Dunes?"

"No. I'm not from around here, remember?" Brian said with sarcasm.

"Watch your tone, fucknuts."

LLANGOLLEN SAND DUNES was a desolate, wooded area close to Emerson River in Southern Dayville. The property was surrounded by woods at first, and then it opened into a wide area of golden sand that seemed to stretch along as far as the eye could see. It was an area only lifelong residents of the town knew of. Kids would ride their dirt bikes on the hills of sand, teenagers and sometimes adults would drive there late at night to share a few drinks and have small campfires.

THE HILLS OF SAND were more visible as Becker drove the car further through the uneven path. He approached a large dirt area and parked the car near two enormous trees. Becker turned off the ignition, and Brian was getting more nervous by the minute.

"Why are we stopping here?"

Becker ignored Brian. They were both looking through the front windshield when they spotted a set of flashing headlights far in front of them. Becker stepped out of the car and paused for a moment. He gazed up at the night sky. It was quiet, and everything was still. Becker walked to the rear passenger side of the car and opened the door.

"Let's go, get out."

Brian hesitated but realized there was nothing he could do.

He considered running but realized that with his hands cuffed and the unfamiliar darkness surrounding him, fleeing wasn't the wisest option. He knew Becker could catch him somehow. As Brian got out of the car, Becker nodded ahead of him.

"Move toward the other car."

Brian turned to look at Becker.

"Look, if you're trying to scare me, it's working."

Becker said nothing. He had no expression on his face.

"I don't know what I've done, but I swear on my life, if you let me go, I won't say a word to anyone. I just want to go home!"

Brian's pleas did not work. Becker nodded for Brian to walk towards the other car. Brian took a deep breath, trying to calm his nerves, and started walking with Becker following behind him.

SITTING IN THE FRONT driver's seat of the other car was Kramer. Next to him was Officer Gus Collins.

Gus had been partnered with Becker since he started on the force as a rookie. Becker took Gus under his wing and taught him everything he needed to know, and Gus absorbed everything he could from the seasoned officer. Gus looked up to Becker, and everything Becker knew was from Kramer.

In Gus's mind, this entire situation was nothing more than a cruel joke Kramer intended to play on the kid in handcuffs approaching them. Gus had seen his fair share of officers hazing suspects during his time on the force and figured this was just another instance of that.

Kramer got out of the car first, then Gus followed. They both stood in front of the car and watched Becker and Brian continue to walk towards them.

When they got close enough, Becker pulled back on Brian's shirt collar. Brian stopped in his tracks and Becker walked to the side of him.

"Stay here, be smart, and don't move. This'll be over soon, and you can go home."

"Just please tell me what's going on. What's gonna happen?"

"Just wait here and try not to look like you're gonna piss yourself."

Becker walked towards Kramer and Gus. As Becker got closer, he could see the smirk on Kramer's face. Becker's eyes shifted toward Gus, who appeared relieved to see him. Becker halted just a few feet away from them and looked at Kramer.

"Was it necessary to meet in the middle of east bumfuck? I can't stand this place." Becker said.

"I like the scenery, gives this whole thing a friendly vibe, doesn't it?" Kramer said.

"Only vibe I'm feeling is my nuts freezing."

"How's our friend?" Kramer asked as he nodded toward Brian.

"The ride here shook him up, I think."

"What did he have to say about Claudia?"

"Claims he doesn't know her. Said tonight was the first time he saw her. I don't know. They looked friendly sitting at the bar, but it was noisy in there, so I couldn't hear shit."

Kramer looked over at Brian, staring a hole right through him. He looked at him and thought for a moment.

"What do you wanna do?" Becker asked.

"We came all the way out here. Let's have some fun," Kramer said.

Becker caught the faintest whiff of alcohol on Kramer's breath, which was unusual since he didn't know Kramer to be much of a drinker. Becker watched as Kramer walked toward Brian, then he followed him with Gus following behind. Kramer stopped in front of Brian, then moved in closer, his face inches away from Brian's.

"So, you're the little prick that's been giving it to Claudia, huh?"

"I swear I did nothing. We just met tonight. I hardly know her, and I didn't touch her in any way!"

"You hugged her, didn't you?" Becker asked in the background.

Brian looked at Becker with a blank expression as Kramer stared at Brian, trying to catch him in a lie. He waited for a response.

"Answer him," Kramer ordered.

"Yeah, I mean, we hugged, but that was it, I swear!"

"You said you didn't touch her, but then you admitted to hugging her. Last I checked, that's still touching. What else are you lying about, kid?"

Brian stood frozen, not knowing what to say without digging a hole any deeper. He finally mustered up whatever courage he had and looked Kramer in the eyes. Brian Tate felt he had nothing to lose at this point.

"Look, I'm telling you what I told him," Brian nodded towards Becker. "I've done nothing wrong. The only thing I'm guilty of is having a drink and chatting with a beautiful woman. I'm not drunk. All I want is to get some sleep and get outta this shithole town and go home. Now stop fucking with me and let me go!"

Kramer looked back at Becker and Gus. Becker smirked while Gus looked unsettled by what Brian had just said. Kramer then turned back to Brian, looking him in the eyes again. He then put his hands out and started doing a slow clap.

"Gotta admit, kid, ya got some balls."

Brian stood still, wondering if he had just made a terrible mistake by having that outburst.

Kramer turned and walked back towards Becker and Gus. He stopped and pulled a flask out of his inner coat pocket, unscrewed the cap, and took a drink. He handed the flask to Becker, who also took a drink, then handed it back to Kramer. Becker looked at Gus.

"Sorry, kid, until you grow some hair on your nuts, you get to stay sober."

Kramer broke out in a drunken laugh. He then handed the flask to Gus.

"I outrank this asshole. I'm ordering you to take a drink."

Gus took the flask and drank from it. Becker then grabbed the flask from him.

"Are we done yet? I'm freezing! Let's put him back in the car and get out of here. I'll drop him back at Terry's and tell him not to mention this to anyone. He won't talk; look at him, he's too scared." Becker said.

"What about Claudia?" Kramer asked.

"You want my opinion? I think the kid might be telling the truth. I think he would've said something by now if he were messing around with her."

"But you sounded so sure earlier."

"Hey, I'm realizing more and more I ain't perfect," Becker smiled. "Besides, I told you it was loud in there, and I couldn't hear anything. At most, it looked like they were doing a little flirting."

"No, we weren't!" Brian yelled out.

Both Kramer and Becker turned to look at Brian.

"SHUT UP!" they both yelled at him.

Brian remained still, frozen with fear. Kramer then turned back to Becker as Gus continued to look on.

"Damn. I was hoping he was the one. Look at him, that smug little prick, thinks his shit don't stink," Kramer said.

"Art, he's not the guy. Maybe you should just confront Claudia about it. Maybe she'll talk." Becker said.

"Yeah," Kramer said, looking into the darkness. "Maybe."

Kramer then reached into his coat pocket and pulled out what appeared to be some kind of blindfold. Becker and Gus looked at Kramer with suspicion.

"What are you doing?" Becker asked.

Kramer ignored the question and turned to walk back toward Brian, stumbling from the alcohol.

"Turn around and face the car," Kramer ordered.

Brian looked at Kramer with a blank expression. He didn't know what to do at the moment. He wanted to run, but he knew he wouldn't stand a chance against three cops. Kramer glared at him.

"Boy, don't make me raise my voice. Turn around."

This time, without hesitation, Brian turned around and faced the car, trembling with fear. All the courage he found moments ago had left. He could sense Kramer getting closer to him.

"Get on your knees."

Brian did as he was told, kneeling on the cold, soft sand. Becker and Gus looked on from a distance. Gus had a nervous look on his face while Becker watched with curiosity. Kramer tied the blindfold around Brian's head, covering his eyes. He then turned around and walked back towards them.

"Alright, fuck 'em, let's go," Kramer said.

"We're just gonna leave him here?" Gus asked.

"Yup! Let the coyotes get him or something. Look at him; they'll have a feast! Maybe he'll get lucky and find his way out, but he's blindfolded and handcuffed," Kramer said with a chuckle.

Becker shook his head and motioned for Gus to get into Brian's car.

"I'll drive," Becker said.

Gus walked over to the passenger side door of Brian's car and got in. He sat there, watching as Brian was still kneeling in the sand, blindfolded and handcuffed. His gaze then shifted to Becker and Kramer, who were still talking.

"We done, Art? Did you get it all out of your system?"

"Yeah, we're good."

"You okay to drive?"

"I got here in one piece, didn't I?"

"Go home and sleep this off, boss. I'll see you in the morning."

Kramer nodded. Becker turned and walked towards the car to the driver's side door. He turned his head to look back at Kramer, who was walking back to his car.

Becker opened the car door and got behind the wheel. He turned and looked at Gus, who seemed to be a little more relaxed.

"You okay?" Becker asked.

"Yeah, now I am."

Becker reached into his pocket to find the car keys. As he pulled the keys out, he also noticed the flask of alcohol that Kramer gave him. Becker inserted the keys into the ignition but didn't start the car. Instead, he unscrewed the cap from his flask, took a drink, and stared down at it.

"Are we just gonna leave him here?" Gus asked.

Becker looked up and stared at Brian through the windshield, then turned and looked at Gus.

"Fuck no. We're gonna follow Art outta here. Then, when he's far enough ahead, we're gonna turn around and come back to get the kid before something eats him."

"Then what?"

"We'll drop him somewhere, slip him some cash for his troubles, and tell him not to mention this to anyone."

"You don't think he'll say anything to anyone?"

"The kid's scared shit. He ain't saying anything. I'll make sure of it."

Becker raised the flask to his lips and took another sip. As he did, he turned and looked out of the windshield. He could see Brian still kneeling in the sand. Becker's gaze then shifted to Kramer, who was now aiming his Smith & Wesson .38 Special at the back of Brian's head.

The gun erupted, sounding almost like a cannon. The bullet connected with the back of Brian's head. Brian's body went limp, and he fell face-first into the ground. He didn't make a sound as he died instantly.

In Brian's car, Becker spit out the alcohol he had just sipped from the flask. Gus's entire body tensed up.

"NO!!" screamed Gus.

Without thinking twice, Becker jumped out of the car and ran toward Brian. Gus followed but paused in his tracks at the sight of Brian's body. Becker stopped and knelt beside it, observing the damage that had been done. A piece of Brian's head was missing from the gunshot wound, the blood seeping into the sand. Becker looked up at Kramer, who stood a few feet away, expressionless. Becker stood up, keeping his hands in clear view so Kramer wouldn't think that Becker was going to reach for his gun.

"Art.... what the fuck?"

Kramer looked at Becker and held the gun up sideways to show him.

"Thing has quite the kick, huh?" Kramer smirked.

"What?" Becker asked in confusion.

Gus hunched over and vomited into the nearby bushes. Kramer glanced at him with disgust, then nodded to Becker.

"The fuck's with him? One minute, he's a tough guy, and now he's puking in the shrubs. Did he get that from you or something?"

Becker continued to stare at Kramer. After a few moments passed, he looked down at Brian's body. He then looked back up at Kramer.

"Why?" Becker asked.

"Had a change of heart."

"This wasn't supposed to happen, Art. What the hell did you just do?"

"Come on, Larry, he was lying his ass off. He's been nailing Claudia this whole time."

"You don't know that!"

"You said earlier you were sure. When have you ever been wrong? You have the best instincts of any cop I've ever worked with; I trust you. Plus, I know the little asshole was lying to me—I saw it in his eyes."

"Art, I told you I couldn't hear what was going on. The kid might've been telling the truth. We don't know if he was the one."

Kramer stood silent for a moment.

"Well, if he wasn't the guy, then you're as responsible for this as I am."

The words hit Becker like a brick. It's true; he was just as responsible for all of this as Kramer was. It was Becker who made the call to inform Kramer about what was happening at Terry's. If Becker had kept quiet, none of this would have happened. Becker continued to stand there, not able to find the right words to say. Kramer's voice snapped Becker out of his brief trance.

"Come on."

Kramer turned and hurried to the trunk of his car.

Becker looked back at Gus, who was leaning against Brian's car, looking away from everything. Becker turned and followed Kramer. As he did, he could see Kramer open the trunk and sort through whatever was in there. When Becker got to the trunk, he looked inside and couldn't believe what he saw. A large black tarp, two shovels, rope, multiple packages of paper towels and cloth rags, and bottles of various types of bleach and cleaning products. At that moment, Becker realized Kramer had planned to murder Brian the whole time.

"Fucking Boy Scout, huh?" Becker asked nervously.

Kramer glanced at Becker and gave him a smirk. He then gave Becker the shovels, the rope, and the tarp.

"Bring this to your car. I'll bring the rest over."

Becker paused momentarily but quickly gathered himself and brought the items to Brian's car. As he approached the car, he made eye contact with Gus, who noticed the shovels and the tarp in Becker's hands. Gus now looked more nervous than ever.

"No way, not happening," said Gus.

"Get in the car," Becker ordered.

Gus watched as Becker dropped the items on the ground next to the trunk of the car. Becker then opened the trunk and looked up to Gus.

"Get in the car NOW!"

Gus opened the passenger side door and got in. As he did, Kramer walked towards the car with the rest of the items. Kramer dumped the items on the ground next to the shovel, rope, and tarp. Kramer grabbed the tarp and spread it out inside the trunk of the car, ensuring it covered the entire interior. He then walked back over to Brian's body. He looked down at the body, then looked at Becker.

"Gonna need a little help here!"

Becker looked over at Kramer, and then he looked at Gus through the car window.

"You stay in the car, don't fucking move!"

Gus remained silent and sat in the car as Becker ran over to Kramer. Kramer had two sets of gloves in his hands. He put one set on and gave the other set to Becker. After he put them on, Becker grabbed Brian's legs while Kramer took hold of his arms. Together, they lifted the body and placed it in the trunk of the car. Kramer then wrapped the body with the extra length of the tarp and used the rope to tie the tarp at various sections. Kramer then closed the trunk. He took off his gloves as he looked at Becker.

"You familiar with Connecticut at all?"

"Been there a few times."

"You ever hear of Quinebaug Creek?"

"No, where the hell's that?"

Kramer ran back to his car and opened the passenger side door. Becker could see Kramer reach into his glove compartment. Kramer ran back to Becker and laid out a map on the trunk of Brian's car. He searched it for a few moments with his finger, then took a pen out of his shirt pocket and circled a small area on the map.

"Here, bring the body here and get rid of it. Guaranteed, no one will find it," Kramer pointed to the circle.

Becker looked down at the map and then back at Kramer, trying to process everything as fast as he could.

"It'll take you a while to get there, but it's a lot of land in a wooded area that no one goes to. You'll be safe," Kramer said.

Becker stared at Kramer, trying to think of what to say. Part of him wanted to take Kramer down right there for what he just did. For a moment, Kramer had an almost pleading look in his eyes.

"Please, Larry, you owe me one."

The words hit Becker hard for a moment, then he shook it off and grabbed the map. He hurried to the driver's side of Brian's car. He opened the door and got one leg in the car when he heard Kramer's voice.

"Larry?"

Becker turned and looked at Kramer, who was still standing at the trunk.

"Thank you."

Becker gave a slight nod and got into the car. He turned

the keys that were already in the ignition and started the car. Gus looked at Becker, then put his seat belt on.

"What the hell's going on? Where are we going?"

Becker waited for Kramer to get into his car and drive away into the darkness. Once Kramer was gone, Becker put on his seat belt and turned to look at Gus.

"We're going on a road trip."

← FOUR

BECKER AND GUS DROVE IN SILENCE FOR ABOUT HALF
an hour. Becker focused on the road, trying not to get them
lost. He also couldn't stop thinking about how the night had
gone. Gus carried on gazing out of the window of the car,
occasionally seeing his reflection in the window.

"What have we done?" Gus whispered to himself.

He kept his gaze fixed outside the window as if it could
help him break free from the horror of what had just happened. Becker looked over at him.

"Try to calm down. Don't overthink it."

Gus glanced at Becker, disbelief etched on his face.

"You ever done anything like this before?" Gus asked.

"Nope."

"I mean, considering we just watched a man get his head
blown off right in front of us, I guess I'm a little freaked out,
that's all."

"Now's not the time to fall apart on me, kid. I need you."

"How are you so calm? For fuck's sake, Beck, after what
we just saw!"

"I've got a good poker face. Truth is, I'm scared shitless,
just like you."

Becker reached into his coat pocket and pulled out the flask of alcohol. He handed it to Gus.

"You're gonna need this a lot more than me."

Gus took the flask and took a long gulp from it. He waited a few moments and continued to drink, trying to ease his nerves.

"Slow it down; save the rest for later," Becker said.

Gus looked over at Becker, and then he put the flask in his coat pocket. Becker looked down at the map, then back towards the road.

"We've got about another hour till we get there. Why don't you close your eyes for a few. You'll need the rest."

"I'm not tired."

Becker shrugged his shoulders and kept driving.

They drove through the darkness for the next hour. Gus's eyelids grew heavy, but every time he blinked, the memory of the blood and the gunshot jolted him awake, reminding him that sleep was a luxury he couldn't afford anymore.

He looked through the window as more trees started covering the sky, and noticed they were driving deeper into the woods. They had crossed into Connecticut a while back, but Gus wasn't sure what town they were in now. After what seemed like an eternity, Becker drove slower through the woods until he stopped. He put the car in park, picked up the map, and studied it.

"This is it. Let's go."

Becker opened the door and got out. The air was warmer, and there was a light coating of fog. He took off his coat and put it in the car, then headed towards the trunk. Gus got out, shut the door, and stood looking up at the night sky.

"I always enjoyed the woods, now I'm not so sure." Gus said.

"Nothing special about it, too many fucking birds. All they do is make noise."

Becker opened the trunk, his breath catching for a moment. The body was still there, wrapped tight in the tarp, an eerie stillness radiating from it like it was just another piece of luggage. Gus walked over to the trunk next to Becker and looked inside. He then looked at Becker.

"No mess. Looks like a rolled-up tent." Gus said.

"Let's pretend that's what it is. Now grab his legs."

Becker gripped one end of the body, the cold stiffness seeping through the tarp. Gus hesitated, nausea bubbling in his throat, before forcing himself to take hold of the other end. They both lifted Brian's body and walked a few yards away from the car.

Becker then stopped and dropped his end of the body, just as Gus did the same. They were out of breath, a combination of heavy lifting and nervousness. Becker stood silent for a moment and looked back towards the car.

"Go get the shovels out of the trunk."

Gus hurried back to the car, got both shovels and walked back. He gave one shovel to Becker, who took it and started to dig into the ground.

"Ground is pretty soft; this shouldn't take long." Becker said.

Gus stood there for a few moments and watched Becker dig. Becker didn't notice at first; he was in the zone and determined to get this done as quickly as possible. Becker then looked up and noticed Gus standing there doing nothing.

"The fuck, start digging!"

"I… I can't do this," Gus stammered, dropping his shovel.

His hands were trembling, and the words felt like they were strangling him on the way out. "I'm sorry."

"Now's not the time for this, kid. Put your big boy pants on."

"I'm sorry, I can't. This is too much. I can't bury a body and just walk away and forget about it!"

"Look, we're in this together, whether you like it or not. I didn't expect this to happen either, but shit got out of control. We've gotta do this and move on. If we do this right and nobody finds out, we'll be in the clear. Now stop being a bush and help me dig!"

Gus stood there for another few moments while Becker continued to dig. He stopped and looked up for a moment at Gus, who at last took his shovel with shaking hands and started digging.

Becker and Gus continued to dig, stopping quickly to take a breather. It took them a while to get the hole to the right depth. When they finished, they picked up the body, placed it into the hole, and filled it back in with dirt.

After putting everything back in the trunk, Gus walked over and stood at the site where the body was buried. He took out the flask of alcohol and had a long drink. Becker walked over to the car and leaned against it, watching Gus.

"What do we do now?" Gus asked.

"We leave, and we forget that this ever happened,"

Gus turned and looked at Becker. He capped the flask, put it in his pocket, and then walked towards him. Becker stood up from the car, preparing in case Gus was going to lose his mind and attack him. Gus then stopped a few feet away from Becker.

"We forget?"

Becker nodded his head.

"I don't know about you, but I'll never forget this night as long as I live. How can you just stand there and say forget it?"

"You got a better idea?"

"What about Art?"

"What about him?"

"You're gonna just sit back and let him do this? Drag us into it?"

"We all played a role in this kid, what's done is done. There's nothing for us to do except forget it; we can't go back and fix anything."

"Bullshit, we can turn him in!"

Becker stared at Gus, and then he turned and looked off into the woods.

"We can't do that."

Gus was surprised by the comment.

"Are you kidding? Yes, we can. We saw him do it clear as day. We can report this!"

"We're not reporting anything, and you're gonna keep your fucking trap shut."

"Why do you wanna protect him from this?"

"We report him, we go down with him, and he knows that."

"We can explain ourselves; we didn't know he was gonna murder that poor kid."

"You're right, we didn't know. But it'll never be that easy to explain. You don't know how far Art's reach is around here. He knows too many people. He's probably busy covering his tracks as we speak."

Gus shook his head at Becker.

"You don't care, do you? About any of this. You just wanna look the other way and pretend like none of this happened, like it's okay or something."

"It's not that. Just trust me on this. We've gotta let it go."

Gus stood silently and watched Becker. He then walked over to the passenger side door.

"You're a piece of shit, you know that? I thought you had some sense of dignity and honor." Gus said.

Becker stood silent and didn't look at him.

"AN INNOCENT MAN WAS MURDERED BY US!!" Gus yelled.

"I know."

Gus wrenched the door open with a force that surprised even him.

"Get me outta here now."

Gus got in the car and slammed the door shut, as if the act of slamming it could silence the screaming in his head.

Becker stood silently for a few moments, then got into the driver's side of the car. Becker started the car to let it warm up, then sat there, thinking to himself.

"Let's go," Gus said.

Becker closed his eyes for a moment and thought about what he was going to say.

"Art took a bullet for me once," Becker began, his voice softer now, almost reverent.

The memory had been long buried, but it slowly clawed its way back to the surface, gnawing at him as he spoke.

"I don't care. Drive the car."

"You wanted an explanation; this is it," Becker said.

Gus didn't react to the words. He sat there and looked out of the windshield into the woods.

"It was years back, before I transferred here. Art came over to the area that I worked in to help us with a homicide case we were having trouble with. Took us a few months, but we caught the guy. Seven people were killed during the time we were trying to catch him."

Gus turned to look at Becker.

"The Hoffman Seven case? I remember hearing someone mention it at the academy."

He waited for Becker to continue the story.

"We tracked the guy to an abandoned warehouse based on a tip from a guy that Art knew. Art and I were the first ones to get there. We broke down the door and looked for him. Fucker was hiding in plain sight with a twelve-gauge pointed right at me. Art pushed me to the side and caught a slug to his chest. The guy ran. I pulled my gun and fired everything I had in the clip. Put seven holes in him, one for each victim he killed. I ran back to Art and called in the shooting, then I sat there with him. I thought for sure he was a dead man. He even had me take down his last words to give to his wife."

Gus kept looking at Becker.

"Then what?"

"The rescue showed up, and we got Art outta there. Tough bastard spent a month in the ICU and got part of his left lung removed. When I wanted to transfer here, he was the one who put in the word to get me in. He treated me like a brother ever since."

Becker looked over at Gus, who was silent and taking everything in.

"We can't report this," Becker said.

Gus didn't know what to say or how to react.

"Kid, I always went to bat for you, and not once did I ever ask or expect anything in return. I'm asking you this one time: give me your word that this won't see the light of day. Nobody else knows about this."

Gus thought it over, conflicted about what to do. He wanted to do the right thing and report this, but he also understood where Becker was coming from. Becker had been like a brother to Gus since he joined the force.

"I'll never forgive you for putting me in this position," Gus said.

"I get it," Becker said.

He shifted the car and slowly drove out of the woods.

"I'm sorry about this, kid," Becker said, the words heavy with regret.

Gus stared out the passenger window, the trees blurring together into a shadowy mass, a reflection of the tangled mess inside his head.

"I have nothing else to say to you," Gus said.

Becker and Gus did not speak to each other for the rest of the ride back to Dayville.

AUGUST 16, 2023

➤ FIVE

THE ALARM CLOCK ON CHRIS COLLINS'S PHONE WENT off at 7:45 a.m. Chris reached over and pressed the side button on the phone to turn it off, then rolled over and fell back to sleep.

Fifteen minutes later, the alarm went off again. This time, after he pressed the side button again, he rolled over and sat up on the side of the bed.

He could hear the busy New York City morning traffic eight stories below. He blinked his eyes awake a few more times, then stood up and went over to the walk-in closet on the other side of his bedroom to pick out his clothes. After gathering everything he needed, he walked to the bathroom to get ready for the day.

Chris was twenty-nine years old, and tall with a thin frame and dark brown medium-length hair. He lived in an apartment at Madison and Forty-Fifth in New York City with his roommate, Gabe Bryant, whom he had met through a mutual friend of theirs when Chris moved to the city, looking for an apartment.

Chris worked as an investigative reporter for the Pembroke Daily, a newspaper covering the suburban areas around New York City. The Pembroke Daily hired Chris after he graduated from Abergele College in upstate New York, where he majored in journalism. It was a fast-paced job that Chris immediately got used to and learned very quickly. Within a couple of months, he was promoted to their I-Team division of Investigative Reporting.

After Chris got showered and dressed, he walked down the hall from his bedroom to the large kitchen in the apartment, passing by the large office that he shared with Gabe. Chris stopped and peeked into the office to find Gabe sitting at his computer and typing away.

"Making coffee, want some?"

Gabe held up his coffee mug.

"Yeah, I'll take a refill."

Chris smirked and continued down the hall to the kitchen.

Gabe Bryant had a heavy frame, with dark blonde hair and a well-trimmed beard. He worked as a computer software engineer in New York City, his first job after graduating with a master's in computer technology from Cardiff Technical College in Smithfield, Maine.

Within a year, he found himself in charge of reviewing other engineers' selected codes, having daily meetings with other management team members, and leading research projects for his team. For Gabe, it was the perfect job.

Chris refilled the coffee maker and made two cups, one for himself and one for Gabe. He then went into the refrigerator and grabbed a carton of eggs and a package of shredded cheese and put them on the counter. He suddenly heard his phone vibrate and went over to check it; it was a missed call from a number he didn't recognize. He put the phone down and went to the cupboard to get a pan.

"Hey, I'm making some eggs. You in?" Chris yelled out.

"If you're cooking, I'm eating!" Gabe yelled back.

A few minutes later, he put the two plates of eggs on the

breakfast nook at the corner of the kitchen, next to the bay window that overlooked the busy city below. He leaned out of the kitchen and into the hallway.

"Get your ass in here. I'm not a waiter."

Chris could hear Gabe chuckling as he made his way from the office to the kitchen. Gabe sat down at the small table and started eating as Chris went to the refrigerator to get a container of orange juice. He poured some juice into a glass, put the container in the refrigerator, and sat at the other end of the table across from Gabe.

"Meeting some friends after work at Rosemary's Deli for drinks if you're interested." Gabe said.

"I can't tonight. I already made plans with Jess. We're gonna try a new Asian Fusion place that opened near Broadway."

Gabe nodded his head as he finished the plate of eggs and got up to put the dirty dish in the dishwasher. He looked over at the refrigerator and saw a piece of paper hanging on it. He studied it for a few seconds.

"I'll give you my share of the electric when I get home tonight."

"No problem,"

Chris glanced at his phone and noticed the time.

"I've gotta get to work. Have fun tonight!"

"Tell Jess I said hi. Have fun."

Chris grabbed his phone and walked to the living room to get his backpack. He grabbed his keys, hanging off the hook with the others, and walked out the door.

EVERY MORNING, for Chris's commute to work, he would walk from his apartment to Calloway Station six blocks away. He would take the train for twenty-five minutes, then get off at Ember Station, four blocks away from the building where The Pembroke Daily was located. Chris would always stop at a corner stand near the entrance for a hot coffee before he went into the building.

Chris arrived at The Pembroke Daily and settled in at his desk at the corner of the office after stopping and talking with a few of his coworkers. He turned on his computer and began checking his emails when a woman walked into his office.

Jessica Bartlett was a little shorter than Chris, with tanned skin and brown wavy hair. She was a couple of years older than Chris and was already working as the head of the I-Team division at The Pembroke Daily when Chris started there. She had been the one to train Chris when he started, and they began dating after about a year of working together. They made a great work team, which was why their relationship status raised no conflict in their professional life.

Jessica walked over to the desk and placed a folder on Chris's desk.

"Got a head start on the Wilton Inn report, where the manager was dipping into the maintenance funds."

Chris glanced up at her and smiled.

"Good morning to you, too!"

Chris stood up as Jessica made her way around the desk. They embraced and shared a kiss. Chris grabbed the folder and opened it to flip through the papers inside it.

"I thought this was getting transferred to Brad. Didn't he want it?"

"He realized he had too much on his plate and asked if we could follow through with it. As if we don't have enough going on."

Chris shook his head and dropped the folder on the desk. He walked over to a table in the corner and shuffled through some of the other loose papers.

"I made reservations for 6:30 p.m. tonight. I figured it's best to play it safe with it still being a new restaurant and everything. I've heard it's been busy there every night since it opened," Jessica said.

"Yeah, that works."

Chris's cell phone went off at his desk, but he ignored it as he was still shuffling through the papers on the table. Jessica walked over to the table.

"Need help?"

"Yeah, that transcript from the interview we did at Mahoney and Wilson last week."

"Already put it in the final report. It's in Sheffield's office."

Chris looked up at Jessica and smiled.

"My hero."

"Speaking of, we've got a working lunch with Sheffield in his office at 12:30 p.m. He wants to go over the Haywood Corp. investigation and make sure we included enough witnesses."

"Wonderful," Chris said as he sat down at his desk.

He looked at his phone and noticed the missed call.

"Anyone important?" asked Jessica.

"Doesn't ring a bell. If it's important, they'll leave a message."

Chris put the phone down and continued checking through his emails. As he did, Jessica made her way over to the other desk across from Chris's and began scrolling through documents.

IT WAS JUST BEFORE 12:30 p.m. when Jessica and Chris began gathering the documents that they would need for the meeting. They grabbed everything and headed down the long hallway, past multiple office desks, to the other end of the building where Sheffield's office was located. Before they reached the office, Chris's phone went off.

Chris peeked at it and noticed the same number from earlier was calling. He ignored the call and put the phone back in his pocket.

"Friggin' scammers," he mumbled.

They got to Sheffield's office, where Chris knocked on the door and opened it for Jessica to walk in first. Bill Sheffield waved them in as he sat behind a desk in front of a large window overlooking the city.

Sheffield was in his mid-fifties, with short salt and pepper-colored hair and a goatee. He had been the senior editor at The Pembroke Daily for almost five years and was trying to position it as one of the leading newspapers in the area. He turned to see the two of them walking in.

"Lunch is on the way. Let's go in here," Sheffield said as he directed Jessica and Chris to an enormous conference table in the room next to his.

They all went into the room and sat down at the table. As Chris was getting everything sorted together, his phone went off. He looked at the phone and noticed the same number was calling again.

"What the hell with this?"

"Will you just answer it already?" Jessica said.

"Sorry, I'll be quick."

Chris stood up and walked out of the office and into the hallway to answer the phone.

"Hello?"

"Hello, may I speak with Christopher Collins, please?"

"Speaking, who's this?"

"Mr. Collins, my name is Detective Jeremy Rivers. I'm with the Dayville Police Department. Do you have a moment to talk?"

"Not really. I'm in the middle of something now. Is it important?"

"I'm afraid so, Mr. Collins. Is Augustus Collins your father?"

Chris paused for a moment.

"Yes, he is."

"Mr. Collins, I'm sorry to have to tell you this, especially over the phone, but police were sent to your father's place of residence early this morning. They found him unresponsive and could not revive him."

"Wait, what do you mean? Is he...?"

"I'm afraid your father passed away. The paramedics that were there tried everything they could."

Chris let the words sink in for a few moments. He stared off into the hallway. The words echoed in Chris's mind—his father was dead. The phone almost slipped from his hand.

He sank into the nearest chair, his thoughts a chaotic swirl of guilt, regret, and the painful realization that any chance of making up for the lost time was now gone forever.

"Mr. Collins, are you still there?"

"Yeah, sorry, I'm still here."

Chris was silent for a few more moments.

"How did it happen?"

"We're not certain just yet, but it looks like he passed away in his sleep. We'll have more information for you when it becomes available if you'd like to request it. Also, I'm sorry to ask this, but is there any way that you can come here to identify the body? There were no other known contacts we could get a hold of; you were the only known family member."

Chris paused for a moment, thinking about the question. He knew Gus had lived a quiet life and that there were no other family members around.

"Yeah, I'll be there as soon as I can."

"Okay. When you arrive, just call me, and I can meet with you to go through the details. Just call me on this number."

"I will. Thank you."

"No problem. I'm sorry for your loss, Mr. Collins."

"Thanks."

Chris ended the call and leaned against the wall of the hallway. He had lots of mixed emotions running through his head. He hadn't spoken to his father in many years. They were always distant with each other, even when Chris still lived in Dayville.

When Chris's mother passed away, he thought that would bring them closer. But Gus always seemed to distance himself.

For a long time, Chris thought that, for some odd reason, Gus had blamed him for his mother's death. Chris and Gus never had the chance to sit down and have a heart-to-heart conversation about everything. Even though Chris had tried a few times, Gus always ended up not wanting any part of it.

After taking a few minutes to collect his thoughts in the hallway, Chris got up and walked back into Sheffield's office. Jessica and Sheffield looked at Chris as he walked in. They could tell that something wasn't right. Sheffield nodded towards him.

"You good?"

Jessica had a look of concern on her face.

"What happened?"

Chris stared at the both of them. He was having trouble getting the words out.

"My dad, he passed away this morning."

Jessica's breath hitched. She said nothing and walked over to wrap her arms around him, holding him as if her embrace could mend the pieces of his fractured heart. Sheffield stood up and put his hand on Chris's shoulder.

"I'm so sorry; I'll give you two some time."

Sheffield walked out of the office, leaving Chris alone with Jessica. She noticed Chris was acting very calm, considering the news.

"Chris, what can I do for you? What do you need?"

"I don't know. I need to leave and clear my head for a little. Is that okay?"

"Yes, of course! Don't worry about all of this; Sheffield will understand. Do whatever you need to do."

She let go of Chris and watched him as he grabbed his items off the desk and walked towards the door.

"Do you want me to come with you?" Jessica asked.

He turned and looked back at her.

"That's okay, but thanks. I'll text you later."

Jessica nodded her head and watched Chris walk out the door. In the hallway, Chris walked by Sheffield, who was getting a bottle of water out of the nearby vending machine. He turned to see Chris approaching him.

"Whatever you need, you've got it. Just let me know," Sheffield said.

"Thanks. I'm gonna have to take some time off to take care of all of this. Is that okay?"

"Of course, take all the time you need. I'll get Brad to come in and help."

"I appreciate it. Thanks."

"No worries. Get outta here and do what you need to do. Don't worry about this place. It'll still be chaotic when you get back."

Chris shook Sheffield's hand, then went back down the long hallway back to his own office to collect his things. As Chris was turning off his computer, Jessica walked in.

"Are you sure there's nothing I can do?" she asked.

"No, I have to pack and head back home to take care of

everything. I've gotta make funeral arrangements and do a bunch of other stuff, I'm sure."

"Do you want me to come with you? Back home, I mean."

"No, but thanks. I'm not going to be there for long, maybe a couple of days.

Chris knew what needed to be done. He was the one who took care of everything when his mother passed away. Gus was too distraught to handle anything.

Jessica watched as Chris gathered the rest of his things. She understood why Chris didn't want her to go with him. He had never met her family, and she knew he had a very conflicted relationship with his father, but he talked little about it, so they left things as they were.

"I'm sorry to leave you hanging like this. Are you sure you'll be alright working with Brad?" Chris asked.

"I'll manage, don't worry."

Chris smiled and hugged her. He walked out of the office and to the elevator, then went down to the first floor and left the building.

During the walk home, his mind was racing with thoughts about what the next steps would be in all of this. What troubled him more was the thought of going back home. Anytime Chris thought about going home to Dayville, he would get hit by a bout of anxiety. Yes, Dayville was his home, but it was also the last place he ever wanted to be.

— SIX

CHRIS WANDERED AROUND CENTRAL PARK FOR A while, his footsteps heavy with unspoken thoughts. The park was his sanctuary, where the city's noise faded, giving him space to wrestle with the memories he couldn't escape. He strolled past the tourists, some of whom he was sure were walking around the park grounds for the first time, judging by the excitement on their faces. He walked through the more rustic parts of the park, areas where he would get lost in the beauty of the woods, forgetting that he was still in the big city. Every so often, he would see someone sitting on a bench offering food to the city squirrels. He walked by and admired the tables that featured different art by the local artists. All these things brought him a sense of peace.

IT WAS JUST AFTER 6:00 p.m. when Chris got back to his apartment. Gabe wasn't there, and Chris felt a sense of relief to have the place to himself. He walked into the kitchen and emptied the dishwasher, then went to his bedroom to pack for the trip.

After Chris finished packing, he went to the refrigerator to look for a snack. When he opened the refrigerator, he heard a knock on his door. Startled, Chris took a moment to wonder who it could be, then walked to the door and opened it. Jessica stood in front of him with a big paper bag in one hand and a smaller paper bag in the other.

"Figured I'd bring date night to you."

Chris suddenly remembered the plans they made for that night.

"Shit, I'm so sorry. I forgot all about tonight!"

"Considering the day you've had, I'll give you a pass."

Chris smiled and took one of the bags from her. She closed the door and followed him into the kitchen. Chris put the bag down, took stacks of takeout containers out of the bag, and put them on the table. He opened one container and leaned over it.

"Smells amazing!"

Jessica placed her bag on the counter and took out the remaining food containers.

"It was crazy busy there. I think this was the better choice. I picked up some extra stuff for you to take with you on the road tomorrow, too."

She took a bottle of wine out of the smaller paper bag and placed it on the table. Chris got two wineglasses from the cabinet and brought them to her.

"I'm sorry about everything being turned upside down at the last minute."

"Are you serious? Why are you sorry? Your father passed away, Chris; you have nothing to be sorry about."

She placed her hand on his shoulder as he uncorked the wine. He poured Jessica a full glass, then hesitated before filling his own as if trying to measure how much he could handle tonight.

"I've got an early start in the morning. Can't get sauced," he smirked.

Jessica watched as Chris finished pouring a glass of wine for himself.

"How are you doing?"

"Okay. I took a walk through the park. It helped. It's my go-to place when I have a lot on my mind."

"If you wanna talk about anything, I'm here. I know you've said you and your father weren't close. But talking about it is better than keeping it bottled up, trust me. My mom and I had a difficult relationship for a long time until a couple of years ago when we finally sat down and hashed things out."

"How did that go?"

"Lots of yelling, lots of tears. But we're much better now."

Chris took a sip of wine and sat down at the table, taking the lid off another container of food. He put the food on the opposite side of the table for Jessica while he opened another one for himself.

"We weren't the type of family that talked things out. If something was bothering any of us, we just hid it. I guess it is what it is."

Jessica sat down at the table across from Chris, and they both started eating. Chris was silent as he ate his food.

"I'm sorry, we can change the topic. I didn't mean to make you bring anything up that you didn't want to." Jessica said.

"No, it's fine. Like you said, good to get it out, right?"

A few more minutes of awkward silence fell upon them as they continued eating. Jessica wanted to ask more and probe him for answers but then decided otherwise.

"How early are you leaving tomorrow?"

"Around 5:00 a.m. Should be able to beat the traffic just in time."

"Are you sure you don't want me to come with you?"

"Trust me, you're better off here. I don't even wanna go myself. Honestly, if it were anyone else, I wouldn't go."

His response surprised Jessica. She wondered how he could have such resentment towards the place that he grew up in. She figured that if Chris ever wanted to talk more about it, he would.

After dinner, they cleared the table, grabbed the bottle of wine, and went up to the rooftop of the building.

The noise of the city was softer, almost like a distant memory. There was nobody around as they sat down in two chairs in front of a gas fireplace.

As they settled in, Chris could feel the warmth of the fire melting the evening's tension away as he listened to the distant city noise.

After a while, Chris's gaze drifted toward the horizon; his jaw clenched as if holding back words he couldn't bring himself to say. Jessica reached for his hand, but she stayed silent, letting him take his time.

"I don't know why I feel like this, Jess."

"What do you mean?"

"My dad. There's a part of me that wishes he were still here so I could have one last conversation with him. The other part of me...is relieved that he's gone."

There was something in his eyes like he was feeling guilt.

"I understand wanting to have that last talk with him, but why are you relieved? Was he sick? Was he suffering from anything?"

"Not that I know of, but I also haven't talked to him in a long time. That's not why I feel relieved, though. It's like I've been carrying this weight—his expectations, his judgments— every single day. For a long time, I just felt like no matter what I ever did in life, it was a letdown to him. Like he was never proud of me, like I was some sort of disappointment to him. And now, for the first time, I feel like that weight is lifted. I don't feel like I have to prove anything to him or that I have to try and impress him anymore."

Jessica could feel the nervous energy radiating from Chris's trembling hand. He had a lot of things that he was holding on to.

"He stopped caring after my mom died. We never got along before that, but since that happened, things only got worse. He became so distant like he wanted nothing to do with me, like I was the one who caused everything to happen. I know I should've made more of an effort over the years to talk to him, but any time I tried, it always ended the same way. He would just ignore my efforts and be even more distant."

"That's not your fault. If you tried to talk and he wanted no part of it, that's on him. You can't blame yourself for things turning out the way they did. You can only do so much on your end. He had to do his part too."

Chris stared into the fire in front of him.

"Do you believe he blamed you for your mom's death?"

"It always felt like it. I guess I'll never know now."

"Chris, I'm so sorry. But I'm glad you're talking about this. Have you ever thought about going to a therapist? I've done it before, and it's the best thing I ever did for myself. I know it's awkward at first to open up to a stranger about your feelings, but it does help if you find the right one."

"The thought crossed my mind, but I guess I've always been so used to just burying my feelings and finding something to distract me that I never considered it."

Jessica cuddled up closer to Chris and rested her head on his shoulders. They both looked at the fireplace, watching the small fire that was keeping them warm. Chris put his arm around her and rested his head against hers.

"Maybe I'll try it when I get back after all of this is done."

"I can give you the number to the one I went to. She's fantastic! Or she can recommend someone to you, I'm sure."

"Or I can just start having therapy sessions with you. It's cheaper, and I don't have to go through that whole awkward part of opening up to someone I don't know."

"If we're gonna start doing that, then I'll have to charge."

"So, what's the rate? Do you accept other forms of payment?"

She hit Chris's arm lightly as he laughed. They cuddled back up and fell asleep in front of the fire. They stayed there for the rest of the night.

———

THE NEXT MORNING, Chris awoke to the fire from the night before still flickering. He also noticed that Jessica wasn't next to him. He rubbed his eyes and looked around the rooftop area, but she was nowhere to be found.

It was still early, and the sun had not yet risen. Chris got up and turned off the fire. He walked towards the side of the building, leaned against the railing and stared out at the city, which was still quiet. He closed his eyes and listened to the stillness for a moment, then walked back into the building and down to his apartment. When he walked in, he could smell cooked bacon. He walked down the hallway to the kitchen and saw Jessica putting a plate of eggs and bacon on the table.

"About time you got up. It's almost 4:30 in the morning," she joked.

Chris was still groggy from waking up as he smiled and sat down at the table.

"I packed food and snacks for you, and your bags are at the front door."

"You didn't have to do all of this, but thank you."

"No worries. I know how much you love saying no to any kind of help."

Chris finished eating while Jessica made a breakfast shake for herself. He took a quick shower, got dressed, and was ready just before 5:00 a.m. Jessica was waiting in the living room when Chris walked in.

"All set?"

"Yeah, pretty sure I've got everything."

Jessica walked over to Chris and hugged him.

"Last chance if you want a driving buddy."

"Thanks, but I need to do this on my own. I hope you can understand."

Chris lingered in her embrace, feeling the steadiness of her heartbeat against his chest. He pulled back and kissed her before picking up his bags. As he reached the door, he turned back one last time; her presence was a comfort he knew he'd carry with him long after he left.

"Be careful. Remember, I'm only a phone call away," she said.

"Thanks."

Chris picked up his bags and opened the door. Just before the door shut behind him, he turned and gave Jessica a wink. Jessica smiled as she watched the door close.

— SEVEN

CHRIS ONLY NEEDED TO PULL OVER ONCE AT A REST
stop halfway through Connecticut to top off the gas tank of
his rented Chevy Cruze. It was just before 9:00 a.m. when
that old feeling of uneasiness started creeping up on him as he
drove past the worn, rusted green sign that said: *Welcome to
Dayville*. He could feel his heart beating faster for a moment,
but after a couple of deep breaths, he slowed it down.

"What the hell am I doing here?"

The town's first traffic light flickered into view. Chris
stopped at the red light and looked around at the old build-
ings that surrounded him. Some were updated, others looked
like they had when he was young. He spotted a yellow sign
next to the crosswalk in front of him reading *Stop for Horses*.
He shook his head.

"Welcome to Hickville."

The light turned green and Chris drove down the road
until he spotted a little restaurant called **Dimitri's Pizza** with
a small sign underneath that read *Open 24/7*. He pulled into
the parking lot, grabbed his laptop bag, and got out of his
car. He looked around and noticed the gas station to his left
across the street and saw the old general store still attached
to it, the same store he remembered riding his bike to when

he was a kid to buy candy. Chris smiled at the thought for a moment, then walked into the restaurant.

In the waiting area, there was a sign that read *Please Seat Yourself*. Chris found a seat in a corner booth, placed his bag in the booth, and sat down. He took out his laptop and attempted to retrieve his unread work emails. Even though Sheffield told him not to worry about work, Chris needed the distraction.

A server walked over to his table, filled his empty glass with water, and placed a small menu in front of him.

"Can I get you something?"

Chris glanced up at the name tag that read **Missy** before his eyes met hers. Her icy blue gaze seemed to pierce through him, cold and unwelcoming. She was slender and of medium height, with dirty blonde hair and what looked to be a tattoo on the inner part of her ear.

"Do you have a Wi-Fi network I can hook up to by any chance?"

Missy rolled her eyes.

"Hunny, this isn't a library. Do you want anything to drink or eat?"

Chris was already doing the math in his head about how much he would subtract from her tip just for the sarcastic reply. He didn't let it show on his face, though, as he smiled back at her. He looked down at the menu for a moment, then back up to her.

"Small meatball and mushroom pizza. Light on the sauce if you can."

Missy scribbled down the order on her notepad, took Chris's menu, and walked away. Chris went back to his laptop, still unable to get any kind of signal. He shut it and took out his phone, scrolling through his emails there instead. After a few minutes, he exited his email app and opened his contacts list. He scrolled down until he saw the name, Detective Jeremy Rivers. Chris tapped on the name and then tapped the call button. After two rings, Rivers picked up.

"Detective Rivers speaking."

"Hi, Detective Rivers, it's Chris Collins. We spoke on the phone yesterday."

"Yes, I remember. How are you doing?"

"Okay, considering the long drive."

"I'll bet. Are you in town?"

"Yeah, I'm just stopping for a quick bite to eat; then I'll meet you."

"Sounds good. I'm just finishing up some paperwork here; then I'll be free."

"Where do you want to meet?"

"Meet me at the morgue at Sterling Hospital. I assume you know where it is if you're from around here. When you arrive at the front desk, just give them my name and they'll show you where to go."

"Yeah, I know it. I'll be there in about forty-five minutes."

"Sounds good. Just shoot me a text when you arrive."

"Okay, see you there."

Rivers hung up on the other end. Chris set his phone on the table and looked out the window into the small parking lot, taking in the scenery of all the trees. Chris remembered coming to this restaurant as a kid with his parents; some of the rare moments he enjoyed from his childhood. After a few moments, Chris picked up his phone and typed a text message to Jessica.

> *"Got into town a little while ago, having a bite to eat, then on to the fun. I'll let you know how it goes."*

After Chris hit the send button, a small tray of pizza fell in front of him, startling him. He looked up to see Missy again.

"Thank you," he said.

"Need anything else?"

"No, I think I'm good."

Missy placed a little piece of paper in front of him and walked away. Chris unfolded it to find what looked like a Wi-Fi password. Looks like the tip amount will have to increase after all, he thought.

Fifteen minutes and an empty pizza tray later, Chris was feeling energized and ready to hit the road. He finished reading his emails on his laptop and then put it back in his bag. He paid the tab, left a five-dollar bill on the table, and walked outside.

He looked across the street to the gas station again and smiled. He put his bag in the car and walked across the street to the general store. Inside, he found that everything looked the same as he remembered. The hardwood floors and the heavy scent of coffee grounds immediately took him back to his childhood. He walked over to one of the candy racks and looked around until he picked out a Cadbury milk chocolate bar. After paying for it, he walked back across the street to his car. As he approached it, he felt his phone vibrate with a text message. He took it out and saw it was from Jessica.

"Be careful, hope everything goes well!"

———

AS MUCH AS DAYVILLE was a typical town in the middle of nowhere, Sterling Hospital was the only place the town was famous for.

It used to be a psychiatric hospital, built in the early 1900s. There had been a checkered history of staff abusing the patients for years until the state and government finally stepped in and shut the whole hospital down for an investigation into the allegations.

Afterward, when most of the staff were let go, the hospital re-opened with new investors and a new medical staff. New additions were added, and over time, it became one of the leading hospitals in the nation, with state-of-the-art technology and research centers.

———————

THE TRAFFIC WAS LIGHT as Chris made it to Sterling Hospital within fifteen minutes. As Chris pulled into the parking lot, he started to get anxious—the memories dragging out from the shadows of his mind, memories he had buried long ago. The last time he was here was to say goodbye to his mother, who had been sick for quite some time but had taken a turn for the worse.

"Just make this quick," he said to himself.

Chris parked the car and made his way to the hospital entrance, taking out his phone to send a text to Rivers, saying he was there. As Chris walked through the main door, he spotted the front desk with two receptionists sitting there and walked over to it.

"Hi, I'm here to see Detective Rivers; I'm supposed to meet him at the morgue."

The receptionist that was sitting closest to him looked up from her computer.

"Go straight down the hall, and you'll see the elevator on your second left. Take it down to the basement level. When you get out, go down the hallway on your left, and you'll see the entrance."

"Thanks."

Chris walked down the hall and followed the woman's instructions to the elevator. He rode the elevator to the basement, got out, and followed the remaining instructions.

When Chris approached the morgue, he noticed a man

standing next to the entrance door, staring down at his cell phone. As Chris walked forward, the man looked up from the phone, then put it away and walked towards him. He was about the same height and build as Chris and looked to be in his early forties, with light brown hair that was combed to the side and a five o'clock shadow. As he approached Chris, he stuck out his hand.

"Mr. Collins, I'm guessing?"

"Detective Rivers, I'm guessing?"

Chris shook Rivers' hand, though his mind was elsewhere, already dreading what lay behind the morgue's cold steel door.

"Nice to put a face to the name. I'm sorry to have to meet under these circumstances, though. How are you doing? How was the drive?"

"It was fine; there wasn't a lot of traffic. I'm okay, just hoping to get this all over with."

"Sounds like you got lucky; I've heard driving through Connecticut is hell these days with all the road work that's going on. They just finished building a bridge or something in New Haven, didn't they?"

"Yeah, looks pretty good when it's lit up, too."

"Nice to know that casino money is being put to good use. You know, after living here my whole life, I still have never been to any of them."

"You're not missing much. It's all older people spending their retirement money and a bunch of overpriced restaurants. Sometimes, the concerts are good if you catch the right one."

Chris was waiting for the small talk to end. Rivers then put his hand out to the door.

"Well, if you're ready, we can go inside."

Rivers pulled open the entrance door and held it open for Chris to go in first. Chris walked in and stood in a small, dimly lit hall. He looked over at a small receptionist's desk to his right, although nobody was sitting there. For a moment, he felt like he was inside a horror movie. Rivers walked up next to him.

"No worries, we can go right in."

Rivers walked down the hallway, with Chris following behind him. He saw one door on his right side, two doors on his left side, and a door in the center at the end of the hall.

"It's the door on the right," Rivers said.

Chris nodded, then made his way towards the door. When Chris got to it, he stopped and stared at the doorknob, then closed his eyes for a moment, trying to calm his nerves as quickly as he could. Rivers stood next to him.

"It's okay if you need a few minutes."

"No, I'm good," Chris said.

Chris opened the door and stepped into the room as Rivers followed behind. As the door shut behind them, they both stood in silence and stared at the table before them. On the table was a white sheet that looked to be covering something resembling the shape of a body. Chris cleared his throat and walked toward the table. Rivers stayed behind, giving Chris the space that he needed. Chris stopped a few feet in front of the table and looked down at the white sheet.

"First time in one of these places, huh?" a voice called out in the distance.

The voice startled Chris from his trance, and he looked to his left. He heard shuffling footsteps that sounded like they were getting closer to him. He noticed a man walking towards him. Chris looked back at Rivers, who nodded that it was okay.

"Thanks for meeting us," Rivers said to the man.

"No worries, it was only my first day off in almost two weeks."

"Stop scaring interns away, and you'll get some help. You should know this by now."

The man approached Chris. He was short and heavyset, with salt and pepper hair that was slicked back. He wore the standard white lab coat with a pair of reading glasses tucked into the coat pocket.

"You must be the next of kin. I'm Doctor Perry."

Chris shook Doctor Perry's hand, surprised by his firm grip.

"Chris Collins."

"Right, over here then," Dr. Perry said, waving Chris over to the wall of pull-out refrigerators as Rivers followed them.

"Doctor Perry is a bit of a legend. He's been here almost as long as the building's been standing." Rivers said.

Doctor Perry waved Rivers off as Chris followed him to the wall and waited as he selected a door to open. After a moment, Dr. Perry opened the door, reached in, and pulled out a table with another white sheet that was covering a body. An uneasy feeling swept over Chris. He looked up at Dr. Perry.

"Need a moment?" Dr. Perry asked.

"No, I'm good."

"Right," said Dr. Perry as he reached over and pulled the white sheet down to expose the face of Gus Collins.

Rivers walked over to join the two men at the table. Rivers and Dr. Perry both looked over at Chris, who stood there staring into the lifeless face of his father. After a moment, he looked up at the two men staring at him. He tried to speak, but he couldn't find the right words; all he could do was nod his head and acknowledge that the body lying before him was his father. Rivers turned and walked to a corner of the room, took out his phone, and dialed a number. He spoke low enough that nobody could hear him. Seeing his father's body hit Chris like a physical blow, leaving him reeling, his thoughts swirling in a haze of disbelief.

"I'm sorry for your loss, Mr. Collins," Dr. Perry said as he pulled the white sheet back over Gus's body.

Chris nodded and watched as Dr. Perry pushed the table back into the refrigerator unit and closed the door.

"How did it happen?" Chris asked.

"According to toxicology reports, it appears to have been an overdose. A combination of Restoril, which is a medication used for sleep, Amlodipine for heart failure, Zoloft for anxiety, Lamictal for neurological disorder, and Advil for pain relief. Plus, he had a blood alcohol content of 0.17."

The news was a bit of a shock to Chris. He never knew of any medical issues Gus may have had. He had never been a heavy drinker, either.

"You don't think he did this on purpose, do you?" Chris asked.

"Of course he did it on purpose," Dr. Perry said. "You don't 'accidentally' take that many medications all at once, then go on a bender. This was suicide."

Chris let the words sink in for a few moments. Something about this wasn't right; he knew there had to be more of an explanation for all of this.

"What do I have to do now?"

"Detective Rivers will let you know. Do you have any other family members that you need to get a hold of?"

"No, it's just me."

"I can give you the number to the local funeral parlor, Simmons & Sons. They're good people and can take care of you from here."

It was the same place that was used for the funeral service for Chris's mother. He even went to school with the youngest son, Matt Simmons.

"Thanks, I appreciate it."

Dr. Perry walked over to his desk in the other corner of the room. As he did, Rivers was walking back towards Chris.

"If you want, you can go to the station and collect your father's belongings. We have the keys to his apartment as well. It's safe for you to go in."

"Okay, thanks."

"How are you holding up with all of this?"

"I'm okay, just a lot to take in. I haven't seen him in a long time. We weren't really that close."

"Yeah, I had an odd relationship with my old man, too. But if it weren't for him, I wouldn't be doing what I do now. Silver lining."

Dr. Perry walked over to them and handed Chris a business card.

"Here's the info for Simmons & Sons; they should be open by now."

Chris took the card and put it into his back pants pocket. He shook Dr. Perry's hand.

"Thank you."

"Take care," Dr. Perry shook Chris's hand, then looked over at Rivers. "See you for the next one."

"Let's hope it's not soon," Rivers said.

Dr. Perry nodded while Rivers and Chris walked out of the morgue. They walked over to the entrance door when Chris paused. Rivers stopped and turned around to face Chris.

"He said it was suicide because of an overdose, but how?" Chris asked.

Rivers stood there, trying to search for the right words.

"Did your father have any history of suicidal tendencies? Did he suffer from depression or trauma or anything like that?"

"No, not that I know of. You're certain it was suicide?"

"On paper, that's what it looks like. The investigation was quick because there was nothing we could find. No foul play or anything of that nature. Your father was clean. It's odd, especially with a reputation like his; he was a cop the rest of us could look up to."

"Yeah, so I've heard." Chris mumbled.

Rivers put his hand on Chris's shoulder.

"I won't let this get out, about the overdose and all that. Your father was one of the most respected officers we ever had, and he'll be honored as such."

Chris nodded, pushed open the door, and walked into the main hallway. Rivers followed behind him.

"I'll let the station know that you'll be stopping by for your father's belongings. There's also a motel close to here if you need a place to stay. I'll be in touch if I know anything else, but it seems like this case is pretty cut and dry."

"Okay. Thanks for your help with everything."

"No worries. You know your way out of here, right?"

"Yeah, I'm good."

Chris shook Rivers' hand and walked back towards the elevator. He entered it and rode up to the main floor of the hospital, then got out and walked out of the main entrance and into the bright daylight, which was a welcome sight after being stuck in a basement for what felt like an eternity.

Chris got into the car and started it; the engine's hum was in stark contrast to the silence that had settled over him. Dayville wasn't done with him yet.

— EIGHT

IT DIDN'T TAKE LONG FOR CHRIS TO GET FROM STER-
ling Hospital to The Dayville Police Department.

He remembered going there to visit Gus when he was younger, but everything was much different now. He stopped the car for a moment, looking at the building. The paint on the outside was new and the bricks showed no signs of wear. He looked at the windows, which were cleaned to the highest standard, as were the steps leading up to the entrance.

The patrol cars parked out front were shiny and new-looking, their exteriors glistening under the weak neon lighting. Chris drove around to the visitor's section of the parking lot and parked the car. He got out and made his way to the main entrance. Once inside the building, it only got more modern. Inside, it was glamorous, futuristic, and way beyond what the outside looked like. They installed security cameras in all directions that were watching the area. There were metal detectors at all the entrance and exit points.

Every table had sophisticated computers, the screens of which were emitting the newest software programs. The walls displayed live feeds and maps through TV screens ranging from twenty to forty inches. The floor gleamed from the light that illuminated the room. It was so clean and professional that it was obvious this was not your typical little town police department.

Chris walked to the reception desk and made eye contact with the woman sitting behind it. Her jet-black hair was pulled back into a bun, and she had the look of someone who would break you in half if provoked. Her name tag read **Officer Ritter.**

"Hi, Detective Rivers told me to come here to pick up some items from the Gus Collins case. I'm his son, Chris Collins."

Officer Ritter studied Chris for a brief second.

"Identification, please?"

Chris already had his license in his hand. He knew better than to reach into his pocket while he was in the police station. He handed his license to her and she took it and scanned it into her computer.

"I like what they've done with the place. It looks different from when I was a kid."

Officer Ritter looked up and glared at him; she was all business and didn't seem to have time for meaningless conversations.

After a moment, she held the license up in front of Chris.

"This says Christopher Collins."

The remark caught Chris off guard. She must have known that Chris was short for Christopher.

"I'm sorry; yes, my full name is Christopher Collins."

After a few seconds, she handed the license back to Chris.

"Go down the hall on the right to the staircase. Go down one floor and check in at the desk on the immediate right."

"Thanks," Chris said as he took his license from her.

She gave a slight nod and went back to her computer work. Chris went down the hall until he saw the staircase, then went down one floor as instructed. He saw a booth behind plexiglass on his immediate right; he assumed this was what Officer Ritter was referring to. Inside the booth was a young man who looked like he was a rookie officer. Chris tapped on the plexiglass to get his attention.

"Hi, the officer upstairs at the main entrance desk sent me here. I'm here to collect some items from the Gus Collins case. I'm his son, Chris."

"Name?" he asked, not paying attention.

"Chris Collins."

"License or any other form of identification?"

Chris didn't realize he would have to show his license again. He reached into his pocket and pulled his license out, then placed it in the cut-out hole in the plexiglass that was on top of the desk. The officer took the license and scanned it in, then studied it for a moment and looked at Chris with confusion.

"This says Christopher Collins."

Must be amateur hour, Chris thought to himself.

Chris took a deep breath, trying not to show that he was getting aggravated.

"My mistake, it's Christopher Collins."

He looked back down at the license, then back up at Chris. After a moment, he gave him the license back. Chris took the license and held it in his hand, just in case.

"Next time, you should state your full name; makes it easier for us."

"Will do," Chris replied, resisting the urge to reach out and choke him.

He walked away from the desk and around a corner where Chris could not see him. Chris waited for a couple of minutes, then the officer returned with a small box that was sealed and a large envelope lying on top of it.

The officer opened the top section of a sliding door next

to his desk and put the box on the counter. He then presented Chris with a form.

"Read and acknowledge this by signing and dating the bottom."

Chris read it through. The document stated Chris had been designated to take the items. He signed it and handed it back.

"Thanks a lot."

The officer nodded his head but did not bother to look up at Chris.

Little prick, Chris thought as he took the box and made his way back up the stairs and out of the station.

When Chris stepped outside, he stopped for a moment, taking the chilly air in his face and taking a deep breath. He got into the car and placed the box on the passenger's seat. His eyes glanced at the top of the box to the envelope, with the edges of the flap well tucked. Chris paused and then ripped the tape of the box apart. He found a set of keys belonging to Gus, a tattered wallet made of leather, and a silver wristwatch. He found himself drawn towards the watch and noticed that the watch face was clean, as if not worn in a long time. After a few moments, he put the items back in the box and started the car. His next stop would be Simmons & Sons' Funeral Home.

JESSICA WAS IN the middle of working out on her treadmill when her phone started buzzing. She looked down at Chris's name on the screen and swiped to the right to answer it.

"Hey, hold on just a sec."

She slowed the treadmill down and then hit the stop button to shut it down. She got off it and walked over to the workout bench, grabbed her water bottle, and sat down.

"Hey, sorry about that. How are you holding up?"

"Well, I've had more fun at the dentist, if that gives you any sign."

"It's not too late for me to come up there, you know. The offer still stands."

"Thanks, but I'm not that cruel to torture you with all of this."

"Busy morning, huh?"

"Yeah, I got something to eat, went to the morgue, went to the police station. You know, fun shit. I'm heading to the funeral home next."

"Sounds like you're getting everything done pretty quickly. It'll be over before you know it!"

"The sooner the better. This place started giving me the heebie-jeebies the second I crossed over the town line."

"Hang in there. Remember, they say time flies when you're having fun," she said sarcastically.

"Don't I know. They told me what the cause of death was."

Jessica took a drink of water from the bottle and put it back on the floor. She then got up and walked into her kitchen.

"What was it?"

"Overdose. Well, suicide is more the term."

Jessica's voice caught in her throat as she stood there, unable to speak.

"Did I scare you away?"

"Chris..."

"Yeah, I know. I wasn't expecting that either."

"Are you okay?"

"I don't know, to be honest. If I had known things were that bad, I would've gone to see him more. Maybe try and help him somehow.

"But you didn't know, and it seems like he didn't want you to know. Whatever it was."

"Yeah, true."

"Don't blame yourself for any of this, that's the last thing you want to do."

"I know. It's just a lot of stuff to take in all at once in a short amount of time."

"I get it. Just try to take things one step at a time. It'll work itself out somehow."

"Okay, Doc."

She rolled her eyes at the comment and got up from the table to get her water bottle from the other room.

"I should get going. I can call you tonight if that's okay," he said.

"Just don't call after 9:00; my boyfriend will get suspicious."

"Lucky bastard."

"Bye."

"Tell him I said hi!"

"Unbelievable." She said laughing.

She hung up as he sat in the car for a moment. He looked down at his phone, smiled, then he put the car into gear and drove off.

––––––––

AS DETECTIVE RIVERS returned to his office at the Dayville Police Department, he noticed the stacks of files on his desk that never seemed to get any smaller. He sat at his desk, leaned back in the chair, swiveled around, opened a cabinet drawer, and took out a pack of gum. It was a habit he had whenever the pressures of the day felt too much for him.

He took a piece of gum out of the pack, unwrapped it, and popped it in his mouth. Once he started chewing, he noticed the tension seeping out of him. A few moments later, he could concentrate.

Rivers turned his chair around, reached over to the desk, and started searching through one stack until he found the one labeled "Collins" that was near the top. He opened the file and started reading it. He started writing on one page, then continued reading. A few minutes later, a knock on his door startled him. Rivers looked up to see Officer Ritter leaning in at the doorway.

"Sorry, just wanted to let you know Collins Jr. came by and collected his old man's belongings."

River's face turned to stone.

"I think you meant to say he collected Lieutenant Collins' belongings. Try to have a little more respect."

Ritter stood up straight.

"Sorry, I didn't mean to..."

"I know what you meant, thank you," Rivers said as he looked back down at the file.

Ritter nodded her head, turned, and walked away as Rivers continued reading the file. A moment later, he heard another knock on his door. He looked up, and standing in the doorway was Art Kramer. Rivers stood up out of respect.

"Come on in, Sir."

Kramer walked into the office and pointed towards the door.

"Open or shut?"

"That depends, sir. Is this a friendly conversation or one where my ass gets chewed out?"

Kramer chuckled at the remark and took a seat in front of Rivers' desk.

"I like how you manage to lighten any mood," Kramer said.

The years were kind to Art Kramer, but he couldn't outrun time. He was older and moved a little slower, but he was still built. His hair was now almost completely grey to complement the short grey mustache he now sported. As he sat down, he leaned to the left and started rubbing his right knee for a moment.

"Should've gotten this thing replaced long ago, but I've just been too busy; at least, that's the excuse I keep telling myself."

Rivers took his seat behind the desk.

"My cousin just had his knee done, and he's only in his late forties. Whatever you're doing, keep it up."

Kramer smirked at the comment.

"Where are you on the Oakland Harbor case?" Kramer asked.

"Close. We reviewed the footage from a side alley close to the crime scene. It shows that prick Cooper tossing the crowbar. We already found the crowbar and dusted it for prints, and it is a 99.2 percent match. I'll have his balls nailed to the door by lunchtime tomorrow; you have my word."

"Good, I was worried for a moment this would get dragged out."

Rivers nodded in approval.

"What else do you have?" Kramer asked, motioning to the open file on Rivers' desk.

"Collins case, just giving it one more look over before I sign off on it."

Kramer sat in silence for a moment, then shook his head in disgust.

"Still can't believe it, just doesn't add up. I've known him since he was a rookie and watched him rise in the ranks over the years. Such a proud man. Not for a second would I ever suspect he would do something like this; such a shame. I've been thinking about it and, proper funds permitting, we should arrange for some kind of memorial for him."

"Makes sense; he was one of the best we had. He was at

the tail end of his career when I started, but I learned a lot from watching him during that short time."

"Have you heard of any funeral arrangements or anything like that yet?"

"Not yet. His kid showed up a little while ago to collect personal items. He was supposed to be going to Simmons & Sons' to settle the arrangements and all that other stuff."

Kramer had a slight look of curiosity.

"His kid, you mean Christopher?"

"Yeah. You know him?"

"Not personally, but I know of him. I saw him a few times when he was a youngster. He would sometimes come to the station with his mother to see Gus. What a peach she was, the nicest woman I've ever met. Tragic what happened to her."

"Sounds like Chris had it kinda rough growing up; he hides it well."

"We're all capable of hiding things when we have to," Kramer said as he looked off.

After a few moments passed, Kramer checked his watch.

"Well, I've gotta run. Let me know of anything new that comes up with this."

"Will do."

Kramer stood up and started walking towards the door. Rivers stood up and cleared his throat.

"By the way, sir, how's the campaign going?"

Kramer turned and smirked.

"Still running unopposed, hopefully, another smooth path to victory."

"It's like nobody has the nuts to run against you or something."

"They don't," Kramer said with a smile.

← NINE

CHRIS ENTERED SIMMONS & SONS' FUNERAL HOME, stopping to let the door close behind him. As he stood silent for a moment, checking his surroundings, an uneasy feeling came over him. The last time he was in the building was for his mother's funeral. Everything inside was the same as it had been before.

He started walking down the small entrance hallway and up a few stairs to what looked like a main lobby of sorts. He turned to his left and looked through the open doorway into a room with chairs set up facing toward a casket at the opposite end of the room. Chris stood there for a moment until he heard a woman's voice behind him.

"Hello, may I help you?"

Chris turned around to see a woman standing in front of him. She was older, maybe in her early sixties. Her long, blonde hair, which was tinged with gray, framed her face, giving her a distinct yet lively appearance. The faint traces of aging contrasted with the modern touch of the blue-rimmed glasses perched on her nose. She looked professional and confident in her black trousers and white shirt, which went well with her toned body. She was attractive for her age, her presence demanding attention.

"Hi, I'm here to look at service options for my father. He recently passed away."

"Oh, I'm so sorry to hear that. I can help you, of course. My name is Mary Simmons."

"Chris, um, Christopher Collins," he said, shaking her hand and making sure he said his full name just in case she asked for any identification.

"Nice to meet you, Christopher. Right this way, we can talk in my office."

She gestured towards the lobby, and Chris followed her. They walked to the other end of the lobby, then up a small flight of stairs to a wide room with three large office desks. He followed her to the desk in the corner.

"Please," Mary said, gesturing towards the comfortable-looking chair positioned in front of the desk.

"Thank you," Chris said as he sat down.

Mary took her seat behind the desk and opened the drawer behind her. She shuffled through it for a moment, pulled out a few papers, and placed them on the desk in front of Chris, pointing out and explaining the different options they had for funeral services, cremations, urns, caskets, and price listings. When she finished, she paused to let Chis think about his options.

"How are you doing with all of this? I know it can be very stressful."

"It's been a lot to process all at once, but I'm good, thanks."

Chris sat in the chair feeling anxious while looking through the papers. Mary took notes as she waited for him. Chris closed his eyes for a moment, keeping his head lowered so Mary couldn't see. When she was done writing, she looked up at him.

"Did your father have any special requests?"

Chris looked up at her and sat in silence for a moment to think it through. To his knowledge, his father didn't have any requests about how he would want to be buried.

"No, not that I'm aware of."

Chris looked at the options for a few more minutes, then made his selection. He thought just a cremation with no wake or funeral would be the best option, keeping things simple. Mary then drew up all the necessary paperwork for Chris to review and sign.

"Okay, I think we're just about finished with everything. Do you have the phone number of the hospital where your father is? I'll call and make the proper arrangements to have him brought here."

"Not off the top of my head. It's Sterling Hospital; I spoke with Dr. Perry."

"Yes, I know Clint well. I'll touch base with him and get everything sorted out," Mary said as she stood up.

This was going almost too easy, Chris thought as he stood up.

"Okay, thank you very much for doing all of this. I can't tell you how much of a help this is."

"That's what we're here for. I can't imagine how difficult this must be for you or anyone in your situation. We want to take as much unneeded stress away as possible, so it's less for you to worry about."

Mary reached into her desk drawer and pulled out a business card, then handed it to Chris.

"I'll be in touch once we have everything taken care of. If there's anything else I can do for you, please don't hesitate to call."

"Thank you," Chris said, taking the card from her.

CHRIS WALKED DOWN the stairs and out the front entrance into the parking lot. As he walked towards his car, he saw a man standing in front of it. The man was older looking, with a gray mustache perched over his top lip, which complimented his well-groomed gray hair. The crisp lines of what looked to be an expensive suit that suggested wealth gave him a striking appearance. His eyes were concealed by a pair of aviator sunglasses, which enhanced his already menacing appearance. When the man saw Chris walking towards him, he took off his sunglasses and approached him.

"I'm taking a shot in the dark here, but is your name Chris Collins?"

Chris was hesitant to respond. The man was very imposing; Chris was almost certain he was either a police officer or someone from the mafia.

"Depends on who's asking."

"Art Kramer."

Chris looked as Kramer extended his hand. He noticed the nice shiny watch, then looked down and noticed the nice dress shoes. A little overdressed for a police officer, Chris thought.

"Are you a cop or something?"

"Used to be. I'm an old friend of your father's. Sorry to hear about old Gus. He was one of a kind."

Chris reached out and shook Kramer's hand.

"Then I guess I'm Chris, but something tells me you already knew that. Otherwise, you wouldn't have been standing in front of my car for however long you've been here."

Kramer laughed at the comment.

"Relax, kid. There's no reason to be edgy or anything. I heard you were here, and I wanted to give you my condolences face-to-face. Gus was a good man, one hell of a cop, too."

"Sorry, I don't mean to come off as ungrateful or anything. It's already been a long day dealing with a lot of things."

"Yeah, from what I heard, Gus didn't have anyone else in his life except for you and his wife. Sorry about that as well."

"Thanks."

Kramer could tell from Chris's demeanor that talking about Gus was a sensitive subject for him.

"I remember seeing you around the station a few times when you were a kid, but Gus didn't talk about you or your mom all that much."

"He didn't interact with my mom or me all that much either; maybe that's why."

"Lots of police officers I've known over the years were like that. They're in the zone while they're on the job, and then they go home, and they don't know what to do, how to separate the things they see, and how not to bring them home with them. Guess that's why a lot of them drink; comes with the territory."

"I'm certain there was more to him than what I saw on the outside. I never asked, though. We didn't share feelings much in the household."

Kramer nodded at the comment and knew not to dig any deeper. He checked his watch, then pulled out a business card and handed it to Chris.

"I know we just met, but if you need anything at all, I'm just a phone call away. Your father was a legend around here, and I respected him, and that respect goes to you as well. If you need anything, just call."

"Thanks."

"Take care of yourself."

Chris took the card and glanced at it, then put it in his

pocket. He watched as Kramer got into his car and drove out of the parking lot. As he watched the car drive off in the distance, he noticed a big sign that was mounted on the front lawn of the funeral home. It had a picture of Kramer on it. Chris read the words below the picture:

Let's move forward. Arthur Kramer for Mayer.

Definitely mafia, Chris thought.

MARCH 30, 1993

➤ TEN

BECKER PARKED THE CAR IN FRONT OF GUS'S HOUSE
and waited for Gus to get out. They had not spoken to each
other for the entire ride back from Connecticut. Gus went to
open the door when he heard Becker's voice.

"Remember what I said? Nobody knows about this. Don't
let me down."

Gus turned and looked into Becker's eyes.

"You let me down, though."

Becker's expression changed, and he glared at Gus.

"Listen to me; you say anything, and we're all fucked. You
don't know Art like I do. If he finds out you said anything,
that's it. I'm not gonna be there to cover for you."

"Don't worry, your secret's safe."

Gus opened the door and went to get out. He looked at
Becker again.

"What about the car? You're gonna get rid of it, right?"

"Don't worry about that. I'll take care of it. You get some
rest and clear your head, kid."

Gus got out of the car and shut the door. He watched
Becker drive off and stood in his driveway until the car was
out of sight.

The first thing Gus did after Becker left was walk to the

nearest convenience store to buy a small bottle of Southern Comfort. He had finished what was left in the flask on the ride back and was still feeling its effects.

When Gus returned to his house, he got in his car and sat alone, replaying the events of the last several hours in his mind. Brian Tate, kidnapped by Becker and brought before Art Kramer, who considered himself to be the judge, jury, and executioner. The crackling sound of the gunshot, the bullet that struck and killed Brian, and Brian's expressionless face staring back at him. Gus would forever remember the images.

His mind was full of guilt that he was trying to shake off. He watched the whole thing happen in front of him, and he was to blame. Despite the chance to take action, he refrained. But what if he had done something? Would he also be lying six feet under the ground beside Brian Tate as well?

He took a drink from the bottle. Despite his hopes, alcohol couldn't erase the thoughts. He gazed at the night sky and sensed a tremor in his right hand. He looked down, and it was shaking. Was he in shock? Was he having a panic attack?

After taking another drink, Gus recapped the bottle. He leaned his head on the steering wheel and felt the tears forming in his eyes. What had he done, he thought.

After sitting in the car for a while, Gus finally decided to get out. He stumbled as he made his way up the steps to the front porch of the house. Janice was a deep sleeper; it would take a bomb going off next to her to wake her up. Gus knew he could just sneak into the house, go upstairs, climb into bed with her, and sleep this whole thing off for a while. Then, he could think things through in the morning.

Gus knew this was the sensible thing to do, but he couldn't bring himself to do it. He stood on the porch, staring at the door, then sat on the steps.

He took the bottle of Southern Comfort out of his pocket

and took another long drink. For a moment, he sat and stared off into the distance, looking at the other houses in the neighborhood.

Gus knew he couldn't tell Janice. As much as he wanted to confess to her his involvement, he knew she wouldn't understand. She loved him, yes, but now that he was an accessory to murder, she would never look at him the same way again.

As Gus sat on the steps, a thought crossed his mind. He got up and walked towards his car. Just as he was about to get in and start it, he realized he had been drinking and had a good buzz going. He put his keys back in his pocket and started walking down the sidewalk, away from his house.

As he walked, the images replayed in his head again. He tried to shake them off, but it was no use. He took another drink from the bottle, but that was no use either.

Gus kept walking until he saw the light-up sign that read 'Dimitri's Pizza.' Something greasy could help sober him up a little. He walked up to the outdoor takeout counter and tapped on the window. An older woman at the register turned her head and approached the window to open it.

"What can I get for you?"

Gus was trying to study the large menu posted behind her, but the alcohol was impairing his vision.

"Just a slice of sausage and olives and a small order of fries," he mumbled, trying to sound sober.

He searched through his pants pocket, pulled out a crumpled ten-dollar bill, and placed it on the counter.

"I'll be right back with your change."

"Don't worry about it."

She shrugged her shoulders and walked away from the window as Gus took a seat on one of the nearby benches. He took out the bottle of Southern Comfort again, noticing it was just under half full. He had another drink, put the bottle away, and waited for his food.

Shortly after, the woman reappeared at the window, carrying a slice of pizza wrapped in foil and a small container of fries. Gus took the food and continued walking.

After about fifteen minutes, he finished everything just as he approached an old-looking house. Gus walked up the walkway towards two front doors. He approached the door on the left and took another drink from the bottle until it was empty. After putting the empty bottle in his pocket, he knocked on the door. When there was no response, he knocked again. Still nothing. Gus then started pounding on the door, no longer caring if he woke anyone else up in the area. He kept pounding until he saw the front light turn on and heard the deadbolt on the opposite side turn. The door opened, and Gus stood there with a blank expression on his face, trying to find the right words to say.

"I'm sorry it's late, but we need to talk," he said.

Standing in front of Gus, dressed in a light blue robe, was Claudia Bates.

ELEVEN

CLAUDIA STARED AT GUS WHILE SHE RUBBED HER EYES.

"It's a little early in the morning, don't you think?"

"I know. I'm sorry, but I don't know where else to go or who else to talk to."

"I'm flattered."

She let Gus in, closed the door, and locked it. She walked past Gus and into her kitchen.

"I'd offer you a drink, but it smells like you've had your fair share."

Gus ignored the comment and walked to the other end of the living room. He felt like he was carrying a heavy burden. He walked towards the fireplace and stopped, listening to the last of the fire crackling. He gazed straight ahead at nothing.

Claudia walked back into the room, the sound of her bare feet audible on the hardwood floor, holding a glass of water and two aspirin tablets in her hand. She stepped closer to Gus and gave them to him, watching him for a long moment as he took the aspirin, then sat down on the couch across from him.

"Rough night?"

Gus stared down at the fireplace.

"To say the least."

Claudia leaned back onto the couch.

"So, are you gonna tell me why you showed up here in the middle of the night?"

Gus looked at her and stared into her eyes.

"Something happened, Claud."

Her expression changed; she stared at him with curiosity but with some worry.

"Okay, do I have to play twenty questions with you or something?"

Gus closed his eyes and looked down at the floor. Claudia leaned forward.

"Gus...tell me."

"You met a guy tonight at Terry's, right?"

Claudia closed her eyes for a moment, assuming where this was going to go.

"Gus, he was just someone I met. Nothing happened, I promise."

"His name was Brian Tate?"

"Yes."

She looked at him suspiciously.

"How did you know that? Were you following me or something?"

Gus looked back up at her again, his eyes meeting hers.

"He's dead, Claud."

Claudia looked at Gus but couldn't find the right words.

"What? What do you mean?"

Gus continued to stare at her, and she realized this wasn't him playing some kind of joke on her.

"What do you mean he's dead? What happened? I told you he was just someone I met. Nothing happened between us!"

Gus tried to find the words, but he couldn't.

"Gus, what did you do?"

"Nothing. I didn't do anything. I should have, but I didn't."

"Then what the hell happened?!"

"Can you please stop yelling? I can't listen to that right now."

"Oh, I'm sorry. You randomly show up at my house in the middle of the night, shitfaced, and tell me that someone I met only a few hours ago is dead. Oh, and somehow, you're involved in it. Forgive me if I'm a little freaked out at the moment."

"Art killed him."

"Wait, what?"

"Becker was watching you and Brian at Terry's. He waited till they closed, and you left, then took Brian in his car to the dunes. I was there with Art. He told me we were gonna meet up with a couple of other cops and have some fun, maybe have a fire and a few beers. I had no clue what he was gonna do, I swear."

"But you said Art killed him. Why?"

"Because Art thought Brian was the one you were seeing behind his back."

Claudia stared at Gus in silence and shock.

"Art knows about us?" she asked.

"No, he's convinced it was Brian, not me. Claudia, I'm responsible for that kid's death," Gus said, tears forming in his eyes.

Claudia stood, her heart full to the brim with unsaid sentiments as she approached Gus. She put her arms around him and embraced him, the comfort he needed.

After a few moments, Claudia withdrew and rested her hands on his shoulders. She stared into his eyes, and she could see the pain he was trying to hide. He looked like he had much more that he wanted to say to her. She could see a tear roll down one of his cheeks. He took her hands away from him and took a step back. Claudia felt she knew where this was about to go.

"We need to end this, don't we?" she asked.

Gus nodded as he stared into her eyes.

"I don't know what to do, Claud. That kid is dead."

"We'll figure this out; you're not gonna be alone in this."

"And Janice. I have to tell Janice about us; I can't hide this from her anymore."

"Gus, I know you need to tell her, but not right now. Too much is happening all at once. What about earlier? Who else knows about it?"

"Right now, it's only you, me, Kramer, and Becker."

"Do you think they'll say anything?"

"I don't think Becker will. Kramer? I wouldn't trust him as far as I could throw him, but I don't think he'll say anything. He knows this is on him, and if one of us goes down, then we all will. Plus, he's the one with the most to lose."

"What do you want me to do?"

"Swear to me you won't tell a soul about what I just told you. I shouldn't have even told you because I swore to Becker that I wouldn't tell anyone. But I needed to get this out, and I had to warn you."

"Warn me about what?"

"Kramer knows you were sneaking around. He's not gonna sit around and let his ego take a hit like that. Just be careful around him. Or leave him altogether."

"That's easy to say. I feel like I'm in too deep with him."

"You have a choice. Don't let him control you!"

"It seems like he can control anyone he wants."

Gus didn't know how to respond to that; she had a point, after all.

"I should go. Claudia, you have no idea how sorry I am about all of this; no words will ever be able to sum it up."

"We'll find a way to get through this."

Gus turned and walked towards the front door.

"Do you wanna stay for a little while longer?"

Gus stopped and turned to face her.

"I can't, but if anything happens, call me. If you can't reach me, you know where I am most of the time. Just ask for me at the station."

Claudia said nothing, giving a slight jerk of her head in agreement. She watched as Gus crossed the hall to open the front door. A thousand unsaid things went through Claudia's mind, but one thing overshadowed them all: she had never told him she loved him. The desire to tell him the words now grew unbearable; the words were on the brink of coming out of her mouth. But he had already decided, and she realized it was the best thing for them both. Even if, at that moment, it seemed as if her heart had just shattered into a million pieces.

Gus looked back at her and gave her a small, wistful smile. She couldn't help but smile back at him and try to put all of her feelings into that single look. The door closed behind Gus, and Claudia went over to lock it. Then she stood there, alone with her racing thoughts.

A FEW HOURS LATER, Claudia awoke to the sound of knocking on her front door. She thought for a moment that Gus had come back. With a sleepy groan, she looked at the time on the alarm clock on her nightstand: 8:47 a.m. She yawned, then shook her head to rid herself of tiredness and got out of bed.

The warm air felt fresh against her skin. When she slipped into her robe, she tied it around her slim waist. She could hear more knocking from the front door as she walked out of the bedroom. The main part of the house was cooler as she crossed from the living room to the dining room, with the light streaming through the windows and reflecting on the floor. When she reached the front door, she looked through the tiny peephole. She paused for a while, her fingertips hovering over the deadbolt. She then turned it and opened the door.

Art Kramer stood there. His face was expressionless as he looked at her up and down. Then he smirked.

"You look even more beautiful crawling out of bed!"

She smirked and opened the door all the way to let him in. He had a cup of coffee in one hand, and a small white bag in the other. He handed them both to her.

"Too early for decaf and a muffin?"

"Thank you."

She took the bag and the coffee from him and walked towards the kitchen. Kramer followed her.

"Have yourself a late night or something?"

"Just a rough night. I had trouble falling asleep."

"Anything on your mind?"

He took a seat at the table as she walked over to the refrigerator.

"No, just the usual stuff."

She grabbed a carton of coffee creamer, brought it over to the table, and sat across from Kramer. She poured the cream into her coffee and stirred it with a spoon.

"Sorry, I thought you didn't like that stuff."

"Sometimes I do, depends on my mood. So, what brings you by so early?"

Kramer gazed into her eyes and studied them for a moment.

"Well, I've been holding it off for a while, and I figured I should stop being such a coward and just ask you," he said as he stood and kneeled in front of her.

Claudia was in shock, not knowing what to say.

"Claudia, I love you, will you please..."

"Art, this is kind of sudden, don't you think?"

"Tell me why you've been fucking other people behind my back?"

— TWELVE

HER BREATH WAS CAUGHT IN HER THROAT. HER MIND began working a thousand miles a minute, but no words could come out. All she could do at the moment was stare back and see his icy gaze go right through her eyes, the tension rising by the second. He smirked at her.

"I know, not the question you were expecting, huh?"

"Art, I don't think we should have this conversation right now. We should talk about this later."

"That's what you think, but I think we should discuss it now."

"Look, we should wait until we're both level-headed. I just don't think now is the time…"

Out of blind fury, Kramer lunged at her and grabbed her by the throat, pulling her off the side of the chair and pinning her against the kitchen wall, knocking the mounted telephone off and causing it to crash to the floor. Claudia cried out in pain and terror, her voice barely audible under his grip that was squeezing her tighter and tighter. Her vision was fading fast, but fear and adrenaline were keeping her from passing out. She dragged her fingers across his arm to pry him away from her, but it was useless. His face was inches away from hers as he pushed her harder against the wall. She couldn't breathe, only gasp.

"Art..."

"You didn't answer my question, darling. Please don't make me repeat myself."

He had a calm but menacing look on his face as he tightened his grip more on Claudia's throat. Her face was turning red; she had tears in her eyes but could barely say anything.

"Art...please!"

Claudia's face turned dark red, and her eyes were closing. Just when she felt like she was going to pass out, Kramer let go as if timing it. She fell to the ground, and all her strength drained from her. She began coughing as she tried to regain her breathing.

Kramer grabbed the chair she was using, positioned it right in front of her, and sat down. He looked down at her as she was still coughing, showing zero remorse.

"I'll wait until you're ready."

Claudia pushed herself up and sat upright on the floor, leaning against the wall. She wasn't coughing as much, but she was still struggling to catch her breath. Kramer was expressionless.

"Are you done with your petty act?" He asked.

Claudia looked up at Kramer. More tears streamed down her face. She couldn't find the words. She was in shock at what had just happened. Kramer leaned in closer to her.

"Nothing to say, huh?"

Fear flooded her when she met Kramer's intimidating gaze, but she wanted to attack him, to hurt him worse than he had hurt her. In the back of her mind, she knew he would overpower her, but she didn't care at this point. As she tried to get up from the floor, Kramer stood up and pushed her back down. She felt weak. Her limbs trembled, and her throat felt like it had been crushed. She could feel tremendous pain in her back from when she hit the wall.

Kramer then kneeled in front of her, his face meeting hers again. He reached out and raised his hand to touch the side of her face. She winced and jerked her head away, swerving her head aside from him, wishing to be away from him. But he kept his hand steady on her face. His voice sounded gentle now.

"Look at me."

Claudia kept looking away from him, not wanting to let him control her.

"Look at me, you whore."

Claudia's gaze turned murderous as she turned and looked at him, like a switch that had been flipped.

"I want you to listen to me because I'm only going to say this once."

Claudia was shaking; she didn't know what his next move was going to be, and she was now fearing for her life but also filled with rage.

"I'll give you twenty-four hours till this exact time tomorrow morning. You're going to pack all your shit, everything you can fit into every bag that you own, and you're going to get out of my town."

Claudia stared into his eyes, and she now felt more rage than fear. She desperately wanted to hurt him for what he was doing.

"You're also not going to mention our little talk here to anyone, understand?"

Claudia did nothing, not wanting to take her eyes off him. His hand gripped her under her chin, and he squeezed. She felt pain but didn't want to give in.

"I asked you if you understand."

He squeezed harder until she couldn't take it any longer, and she nodded her head.

"Good."

He let go of her and leaned in closer to her.

"You hurt me in a way that I've never experienced before, and I can never forgive you for that. So, I want you to remember these words…"

He got closer so that his mouth was almost touching her ear. Then he whispered.

"If I see you in this town again, I don't care if you're just visiting or passing through, I'll kill you."

The words felt like a gut punch to her; even after everything that had just happened in the last few minutes, she couldn't believe the words he had just said to her.

"Do you understand me?"

She nodded. She was speechless at this point.

"Good."

He stood up, grabbed his coffee from the table, and walked towards the front door. Claudia sat on the floor and watched him leave. He then stopped and turned his head towards her.

"When I come back tomorrow, I expect you to be gone."

Kramer stared down at Claudia, who was still on the floor. Then, without saying another word, he turned and walked out the front door, shutting it behind him. His footsteps became softer the further he walked away from the house.

All the pent-up emotions she had been holding back hit her at once. The anger and despair that she suppressed flooded her. She sat still on the floor while tears rolled down her face.

AUGUST 17, 2023

━ THIRTEEN

IT WAS MID-AFTERNOON WHEN CHRIS PULLED INTO the driveway of Gus Collins' apartment. He got out of the car and walked over to admire the view of Creekwood Lake, which was the only thing he ever enjoyed about the place. The view was always magnificent. Chris stared out at the lake for what seemed like an eternity. He recalled when he was a kid, Gus would take him fishing in his old rowboat out on the other side of the lake, where Gus had once owned a piece of land.

At first, Chris would visit Gus during holidays, but their relationship soon deteriorated, and Chris stopped visiting altogether.

Chris shook off the memories and made his way to the back entrance of the building. He opened the door and climbed the stairs to the second floor, the familiar smell of the wooden floors hitting him like a brick. Standing in front of Gus's apartment door, Chris took out the keys and unlocked it. He took a deep breath, exhaled, and then opened the door.

When Chris stepped into the living room, it felt like he had traveled back in time. Everything looked the same as it always had. The rugs, the furniture, the curtains, all in the same spots. Nothing had changed. Even the smell of the apartment was unchanged; the faint scent of cedar wood still hung in the air after all these years. Gus had always been a creature of habit, disliking any form of change in his personal life.

Chris walked around the living room, seeing the random photographs on the walls of various landscapes that Gus had taken over the years. Chris remembered Gus used to enjoy taking photographs, one of the few things that seemed to bring him joy. He walked past the old record player and noticed the small stack of records next to it. He then made his way into the kitchen. Like the living room, the kitchen stayed the same as it always had, except for what appeared to be a newer gas stove—nothing fancy.

Chris walked down the hallway, past the bathroom, and into Gus's bedroom. It was still the same, except for the new sheets and blankets on the bed.

Chris looked at the nightstand next to the bed and saw the picture of his mother, Janice. He picked up the picture and studied it for a while. Not a day went by that he didn't think about her. They had always been close; their relationship was more like that of best friends than mother and son. Chris then felt a rush of sadness come over him; he still missed her.

He put the picture back on the nightstand and then saw the small drawer under the tabletop. Chris tried to open it, but it was locked. He took the set of keys from his pocket and tried each one on the drawer, but none worked. Frustrated, he gave up and walked out of the bedroom and back to the living room.

He walked back into the kitchen and looked around, noticing the aged refrigerator. He opened it and looked inside, then closed it and walked over to the window, looking out at the lake again. He opened the window and closed his eyes, listening to the birds and the sounds of the choppy water flowing up against the dock.

After a few minutes, he closed the window and walked back into the living room. He walked over to a baker's rack that he spotted in the corner of the room and looked through the small pile of papers that were on it. Nothing seemed out of place. He then noticed that on one of the bottom racks, there was a photo album. Chris took the album and sat down on the couch. He opened the album and saw photographs Gus must have taken over the years of different nature scenery.

The beauty of the pictures amazed Chris. Some were of different sunrises and sunsets, a few pictures of waterfalls from what looked to be different hiking trails, and some close-up pictures of birds. When he was finished looking through the rest of the album, Chris stood up and put the album back on the rack. After taking one last look around, he decided it was time to leave. Chris locked the front door, then made his way downstairs and out to the driveway. As he stepped outside, he noticed a black Toyota Camry pulling out of the driveway and onto the main road.

He didn't remember seeing any other cars when he arrived, and he hadn't been in the apartment for long. Chris shrugged it off and got into his car.

Although Chris wasn't much of a drinker, he felt he deserved a beer after the day he had. So, he stopped at the only place he knew that had good food and drinks: Terry's Restaurant, formally known as Terry's Friendly Tap.

Chris pulled into the parking lot and looked at the building. From the outside, Terry's looked the same, aside from a new roof and what looked like vinyl siding replacing the old wooden panels. Chris remembered hearing that Terry's, for many years, had been a hangout for local cops to drink at. He always remembered it as the family restaurant that stood before him.

Chris got out of the car and walked into the restaurant.

The interior looked updated, but the layout was still the same as he remembered. To his left was the open dining area, and to his right was the bar. He went over and took a seat at the bar. Chris noticed that one of the many TVs mounted on the upper section of the bar was showing a Boston Red Sox game.

The Red Sox were playing the Kansas City Royals at Fenway Park, America's oldest ballpark, and home to the Red Sox. The score was Sox–3, Royals–2. It was the bottom of the fifth inning with plenty of game left to play.

Even though Chris lived in New York, he was a Red Sox fan through and through. His mother was also an avid Red Sox fan, and her enthusiasm had rubbed off on him at a young age. Baseball was about the only sport he had any interest in.

Chris noticed the bartender approaching out of the corner of his eye. The bartender looked to be younger than Chris, with a thin build. He wore a plain black t-shirt and a Red Sox hat, which he wore backwards.

"Hey there, what can I get for you?" the bartender asked.

"Do you have any Sam Adams on draft?"

"Sure do, seasonal or regular?"

"I'll take regular, please."

"Twelve-ounce or a tall boy?"

"Come again?"

The bartender shook his head and smirked at Chris's question.

"Twelve-ounce glass or twenty-four-ounce glass?"

"Twelve-ounce, please."

"You got it."

The bartender grabbed a clean glass from the freezer underneath the bar, walked over to the tap, and poured. After a moment, he walked over to Chris and placed the beer in front of him.

"Starting a tab?" the bartender asked.

"No, just one and done."

"Wanna look at a menu or anything?"

Chris thought for a moment and gave in.

"Do you still have the sweet barbecue wings, the boneless ones?"

"Of course, those'll never go away," the bartender said with a smirk.

"I'll take an order of those, thanks."

"Got it."

The bartender left to place the order while Chris continued to watch the ball game and sip his beer. He watched as one player for the Royals hit a 2-run home run right out of the park. Chris shook his head and took another sip of his beer. Someone slammed their hand down on the bar top, startling Chris. Then he heard a loud voice.

"Fuckin' Sanders!"

Chris turned and saw a man take a seat at the bar next to him. The man was older, not heavyset, but also not the type who looked like he went to the gym often. He had thinning salt-and-pepper hair that matched his goatee. He was looking up and yelling at the TV.

"I keep saying the Sox paid way too much for that arm, and every time that worthless sack of shit pitches, he proves me right."

Chris could not help but chuckle a little at the comment. The man turned to look at him.

"Sorry, shit just gets old after a while. I don't know how that team hasn't gone bankrupt yet with all the cash they spend on these shit players. They could put the old-timers like Ortiz and Martinez out there now, and they would still play better than these kids. Hell, they'd run circles around them!"

"So, we should wait another eighty-six years for the next championship?" Chris asked.

"Fuck no! Get rid of the owners and start from scratch. Time for a rebuild!"

Chris found this to be the most enjoyable conversation he'd had all day. He then noticed the bartender walking back over to him with a plate of barbecue chicken. The man studied the bartender's appearance.

"Will you turn your hat around? You look like a fuckin' toolbag."

"Nice to see you too," the bartender replied as he put the plate in front of Chris.

The man studied the plate of chicken, then gave Chris a look of warning.

"Hope you brought wet wipes with you; your asshole's gonna be on fire after eating that stuff," the man said, eying the plate of chicken.

"Those aren't the hot wings, Larry," the bartender said as he walked away.

The man leaned over and whispered to Chris.

"Never mind, you're good then."

The bartender came back over with a cold twelve-ounce glass of beer and placed it in front of the man.

"You'll have to get used to old Larry here quick. There's not much of a choice," the bartender said to Chris.

The man raised his middle finger at the bartender, who responded by blowing him a kiss. The man shook his head.

"Smartass kid. If I were ten years younger and thirty pounds lighter, I'd kick the shit outta him."

Chris kept laughing at the stranger sitting next to him, who extended his hand out.

"Larry Becker."

"Chris Collins."

Chris shook Becker's hand. Becker nodded, then turned to look up at the ball game on the TV.

"You from around here, Chris Collins?"

"Used to be. I live in New York now."

Becker turned and gave Chris a stern look.

"Please tell me you're not a Yankees fan."

Chris lifted his hands up.

"Red Sox fan for life."

"Good. Otherwise, I'd have to kick you in the nuts and steal your chicken," Becker said, nodding toward the plate in front of Chris.

"After you lose thirty pounds, right?"

"You catch on quick, Chris from New York," Becker said, raising his glass to him.

Chris pushed the plate of chicken towards Becker.

"Care for some?"

"Thought you'd never ask."

Becker took a piece of chicken as they both watched the game.

"So, Chris from New York, what brings you back to our charming little town?"

"Taking care of some family stuff. My father passed away, so I'm handling the arrangements, or trying to, I should say."

Becker raised his glass to Chris.

"Condolences."

"Thanks."

Chris took a sip from his glass as Becker watched the game for a moment, then he turned to Chris with curiosity.

"Any relation to Gus Collins?"

"Yup, he was my father."

Becker leaned back in his chair.

"No shit? Small world, after all. He was a good guy."

"That's what everyone seems to say. Did you know him too?"

"We worked together for a little bit."

"So, you're a cop, too?"

"Was. I'm retired now."

"Must be nice, huh?"

"It has its perks. I get to sit here, drink all day and bother that little shit stain," Becker said, nodding toward the bartender.

Chris raised his glass.

"To living the dream."

Becker raised his glass and downed the rest of his beer.

"So, how was old Gus in his later years? He was still on the job when I left."

"I guess he was happy. I didn't really see him all that much, we sort of drifted apart."

Becker nodded as he waved to the bartender for another beer.

"Well, he couldn't have been that happy if he offed himself."

The comment took Chris by surprise. He looked at Becker with confusion.

"How the hell did you know that?"

Becker stared at the TV, ignoring the question.

"Are you going to answer me, or do I have to stop sharing my chicken?"

"Kid, I may be retired, but people still talk."

Chris stared at him for a moment. He hesitated for a moment about whether to ask more questions.

"So, if you know what happened, do you know why he would've done it?"

Becker reached over and took another piece of chicken off Chris's plate.

"Nope, didn't talk to him much after I left. From what I heard, he left not long after I did and didn't keep in contact with anyone. Then again, he was always like that, quiet."

Chris stared at his beer for a few moments. So many thoughts ran through his mind.

"It doesn't make any sense. Something's not adding up."

The bartender brought over a freshly poured glass of beer for Becker. Becker took it and looked at Chris.

"When did you become a detective?"

"I'm not. I'm a reporter."

"No shit. Guess that's close enough."

Becker took a sip of his beer, and both men sat in silence for a few more minutes. Becker sighed and leaned towards Chris.

"Look, if you're any good at what you do, then you know enough to go snooping around. I'm guessing you've got access to your old man's place. Try digging around there and see if anything turns up."

"I already tried that."

"Try harder."

Chris turned and gave Becker a stare as if silently asking him if he knew anything.

"What, you afraid you might find something? Skeletons in the old man's closet?"

"No, just... I don't know. What do you think? You knew him, too; you guys must've gone back pretty far. What was he like to you? Did he ever seem off or anything over the years?" Chris asked.

"The fuck is this quiz time? No, I don't know what he was like in his personal life; none of my business."

As Becker stared back at the TV and continued watching the ball game, Chris reached into his pocket, took out thirty dollars, placed the money on the table, and then got up from his seat. Becker looked over at him.

"Did I scare you off? I have that effect."

"Gonna take your advice and go snooping around. Care to join me?"

Becker took the last piece of chicken from the plate.

"Retired."

Chris stuck his hand out towards Becker.

"Thanks, whatever it's worth."

Becker stared back at Chris and shook his hand.

"Keep your eyes open, especially around here."

Chris nodded and walked out. He got into his car, and as he pulled out of the parking lot, he noticed the same car he had seen earlier at Gus's place, a black Toyota Camry.

Must be an admirer. He thought.

FOURTEEN

THE SUN WAS SETTING AS CHRIS PARKED THE CAR AT Gus's apartment, and the faint orange light of the evening painted the deserted road. He looked around to make sure he wasn't followed.

The stairs were quite old, making loud creaking sounds with every step he took. He groaned and protested as he climbed up to the second floor of Gus's apartment. He stood in front of the door, reached into his pocket, and took out the keys. Once he entered, he closed the door and locked it behind him. The apartment was dim. Chris turned on a few lights and looked around.

The first room was the living room. He searched the room by opening drawers and cupboards and going through items. All that was there for him to find were some old utility bills and a stack of junk mail.

Next was the kitchen, then the bathroom. Chris searched all the drawers and cabinets. Again, nothing. Chris walked down the hallway and into the first bedroom, which Gus used as an office. He had the feeling he might find something here; it made sense that Gus would hide something here. But the desk and its drawers were empty.

Impatience set in as he walked down the hall to Gus's

bedroom at the end of the hall. The next area of focus was a small walk-in closet, but again, nothing. He grew irritated as he started looking through Gus's belongings underneath the bed and in the dressers. Nothing.

Chris turned his attention to the side table, which was positioned near the bed. The small drawer that had failed to open earlier. He tried to open it again, but no luck.

Chris's cell phone started ringing. The sound startled him, and he shuffled around in his pocket to get the phone. He looked at the screen, and it was a number he didn't recognize. He swiped and answered it.

"Hello?"

"Hi, Mr. Collins? It's Mary Simmons from Simmons and Sons. I wanted to let you know we should have everything ready by tomorrow afternoon for you to pick up."

Chris kept trying to open the drawer under the side table.

"Okay, thank you."

"How are you doing with everything else?"

Chris wanted the conversation to end so he could focus on getting the drawer open.

"Oh, you know, just grieving and all that stuff."

Chris pulled the drawer handle and banged on the table-top, hoping it would somehow open the drawer.

"Okay, well, if there's anything else that you need, you know where to reach me."

"Appreciate it. Have a good rest of the night."

"You too."

Chris hung up the phone, already feeling nervous in his chest. He had to open that drawer. He had a feeling something important was in there. Otherwise, why would it still be locked? He needed the right tool. He weighed his choices as quickly as possible. A sledgehammer would get the job done, but where would Gus have stored something like that? The basement, he thought.

Chris exited the apartment and slid down the stairs toward the ground floor. While walking, he observed the door that lead to the basement. He tried the knob, pulling it towards him and turning it. The door opened, and he stepped inside and looked around the room, lit only by a faint light, which revealed a staircase that didn't look very wide. As he walked down the stairs, the air turned frigid with a stench of mold that mixed with laundry detergent.

He proceeded to the bottom of the stairs. After flicking the switch beside the door, a large area lit up before him. He eyed the small wet bar with wine bottles and glasses in one corner, with boxes stacked up to the ceiling along one part of the wall, and a washer and dryer unit on the other side of the room. But there were no tools. Chris searched through all the boxes that contained old clothes, papers, and other gadgets. He hoped to find what he was looking for, but to no avail. Irritated, he walked back up the stairs. At the top, he looked through the window of the house and saw an old, rusty shed in the backyard. It was on the verge of crumbling, but he was running out of places to search.

He ran through the entrance doorway and around the house. Chris charged toward the other side where the shed was located.

The door groaned when he pushed it open. He entered the structure, pulled a string beside a single light bulb, and lit the room. Chris saw every hand tool he could think of hanging on the walls. He grabbed a thick metal hammer and thought that would do.

He shut the door of the shed and turned to walk back to the house when he heard a ringing sound from something that he had kicked to the side. Curious, Chris looked down at the ground and started searching the area. He then noticed something with a faint shine that caught his eye. A key. Chris picked it up and studied it, and he knew right away.

"Thanks, Dad."

Chris's heart raced as he dashed back to the apartment, the sound of his breathing chasing him up the stairs to the second floor. His heart started beating faster as he rushed into Gus's bedroom to get to the side table on the right. He took the key, now warm from being held in his hand for quite some time, and slipped it into the keyhole of the drawer. He stopped breathing as he twisted it, and he could hear the turning click.

The drawer pulled open to display what was inside it. He looked through the drawer with disappointment setting in his heart. There was nothing there but a folded-up piece of paper. He threw the key and the hammer to the floor, then fell on the edge of the bed. A storm of thoughts and questions began in his head.

He had looked everywhere in the apartment and could find nothing. Could it be that the police had visited the scene earlier and carted away anything that could be of any use? The thought plagued him, but he did not find a way of solving it. Chris looked at the time and saw how much of the night had elapsed. Going back to the police station now was of no purpose.

His eyes went back to focusing on the opened drawer where the piece of paper was. After a few moments of hesitation, he extended his arm and picked up the paper. As he did, he saw a photo that was hidden underneath it. He took the photo and studied it for a moment, then put it down and unfolded the paper.

It took a few minutes for the words to sink in. Chris read the note again and found that the words became clearer, as if the repeated reading made them deeper. He put the paper down and looked at the photo again, and then he noticed his hands were shaking.

He felt a chill run down his spine as he set his gaze on the drawer. The room seemed to close in around him, the air growing thick with an unnameable dread. Chris looked as though he had seen a ghost, his face drained of color, his expression one of complete and utter shock. The discovery he had just made was far more disturbing than anything he had imagined.

MARCH 30, 1993

— FIFTEEN

JANICE COLLINS AWOKE AFTER 8:30 A.M. SHE TURNED over and draped her arm over the space on the bed where Gus would usually be, but he wasn't there.

The sunlight streamed through the bedroom window, piercing her gaze. She rolled over to her side of the bed and sat up. She ran her hand through her wavy light red hair. The sun was away from her eyes now, and she looked out the window for a moment, taking in the clear, bright morning. She got up and walked over to her closet to get her robe. She slid her feet into her slippers and walked out of the bedroom, down the small corridor, and into the open sunroom. She walked to the side door and opened it. After she picked up the morning paper, she stood still for a moment, letting the warm morning breeze cover her face. She then shut the door and walked to the kitchen.

When she entered the kitchen, she found Gus sitting by himself at the table, his head slumped down on it. When she walked over and opened the refrigerator door, the noise woke him. She looked over.

"How long have you been down here?"

"I don't know. I got home late and went to have a snack before bed. I must've just fallen asleep."

Janice shook her head as if this was typical. She searched in the refrigerator for a container of coffee grounds, then took it over to the counter where the coffeemaker was. She plugged it in and switched on the power. Gus remained at the table, rubbing his eyes and trying to wake himself up.

"Another rough night at work?" Janice asked.

"Yeah."

She filled the coffeemaker's water container, poured a few scoops of coffee grounds into it, closed the lid, and turned it on. As the coffee brewed, she walked to the table and took a seat across from Gus.

"Anything you wanna talk about?"

Gus sat there and looked at her for a while, struggling to find the words. He knew there would not be an easy way to do this, but there was no other choice. He had to tell her about his affair with Claudia. His eyes started to fill with tears.

"Janice..."

Janice reached out, grabbed Gus's hands, and held them tight.

"It's okay, it's okay to talk about it. You've been so distant for a while. Maybe you should take some time off. Give yourself some time to clear your head?"

"It's not that."

"Then what is it?"

"So much has happened. I don't know what to do, how to figure it all out."

"It's okay, I'm right here. You can tell me anything. I promise I'll do whatever I can to help you through it."

Gus pulled his hands away from hers.

"Janice, this isn't going to be easy."

"Talk to me, Gus. What is it?"

"I love you..." Gus said.

"I love you too."

"Janice, there's someone else."

She looked confused, the words not sinking in right away. After a moment, she stood up from the table and walked back over to the counter where the coffeemaker was. She opened the cabinet above her, grabbed a coffee cup, filled it, and stood there in silence.

"Another woman?" she asked.

"Yes."

Janice closed her eyes and tried to process everything.

"How long?" she asked.

"A couple of months."

There was silence between them for another few moments. Janice lowered her head, looking down at the counter.

"How did you meet her?"

"She came into the station asking for a VIN check on a car she just bought."

"And then?"

"We talked for a while. She asked if she could buy me a coffee as a thank you for helping her out."

"So, she asked you out, and you accepted."

Gus didn't have a response; he just lowered his head and continued to look at the tabletop. She couldn't bring herself to look at him yet.

"Anything else you'd like to share?"

Gus didn't even want to think about the recent events that happened in the last twenty-four hours; admitting to the affair was already bad enough.

"No."

Janice stood there, her back still turned to Gus.

"I can't tell you how sorry I am, Janice."

"You're not sorry. If you had slept with her just once, then maybe an apology would make sense. But for months? No, there's no apology for that."

"There's no excuse for what I did. I wasn't thinking right. I don't know what was going on."

"Something else was doing the thinking for you." She said coldly.

Gus sat in silence, not knowing what else to say.

"I'm pregnant," Janice said with anger as she turned around to finally face Gus. Her eyes were like daggers.

Gus looked up in shock at what he had just heard.

"You are?"

"Yes."

Tears rolled down Gus's cheeks. Janice took her coffee and walked past Gus. He heard her enter the bedroom and close the door behind her. There was nothing he could do for the moment; Gus couldn't believe how much damage he had just caused in his life.

GUS HEARD THE KNOCK at the front door from the basement. He had spent the rest of the day down there re-organizing his tools and boxes of possessions he had collected over the years. He cleaned all the shelves that were mounted on the walls. He was doing anything he could to take his mind off everything running through it. Whoever was at the door, their company, would be welcome at this point.

Gus switched off the lights and climbed the stairs. He glanced around but didn't see Janice. He assumed that she was still in the bedroom where she had stayed for most of the day. He walked to the front door and opened it, and he was stunned into silence. Standing before him was Claudia. She was wearing slim jeans and a hooded sweatshirt, with a scarf around her neck and wide sunglasses.

"I'm sorry; I didn't know where else to go or who to talk to."

Gus stepped outside, leaving the door open behind him. "What is it?"

She stood for a moment in front of Gus, searching for the right words to say.

"I'm leaving. I'm not sure where, but I have to get out of here."

"What happened?"

"It's not important. Art knows everything, and it's better for everyone if I just leave," she said, her voice cracking.

Gus felt a rush of fear run through him; Claudia could see it on his face.

"He doesn't know about you or that it was you. He's still convinced it was Brian."

Gus could see what looked like the top of a bruise on Claudia's neck. He reached out and pulled the scarf down, exposing part of the long, dark bruise that took up most of her neck.

"What did he do to you?"

Claudia pulled the scarf back up to cover it.

"Don't worry about it. It's all over, and that's what's important."

Gus looked at her and felt helpless, but he also felt anger at what had happened to her.

"Look, Gus, before I go, I just want you to know…"

Suddenly, they both heard Janice's voice.

"You must be the home wrecker."

Gus turned around, and both he and Claudia saw Janice standing at the end of the hallway. Claudia looked at Gus with surprise.

"You told her?"

"Yes, he did," Janice said as she walked closer to the doorway.

Claudia took a few steps back as Janice approached.

"Listen, I don't want any trouble. I know I've already caused enough as it is."

"Good, you're not as stupid as you look," Janice said.

Gus avoided eye contact with both women. He was standing in the middle and was ready to separate them if he had to.

"So, you're leaving, I hear?" Janice asked Claudia.

"Yes."

Janice looked at Gus, waiting for him to look her in the eyes.

"Well, looks like you have a choice to make: her or me."

Gus looked at Janice, then at Claudia.

"I just want you to know, it doesn't matter who you choose; you will never share the same bed with me again," Janice said.

Janice turned and walked back to the bedroom, shutting the door behind her. Gus looked down at the now empty hall, then back at Claudia.

"You don't have to say it. We already agreed, remember?" Claudia said.

"She's pregnant. I can't do this to her. She's already been through enough. I wanna try to work things out with her."

Gus could see the tears rolling down Claudia's cheeks.

"You're making the right choice," Claudia said.

She turned and walked away from the house. Gus watched her get into her car and drive away. He stood at the doorway staring into the distance, then turned and walked back into the house, shutting the door behind him.

← SIXTEEN

GUS LOOKED OUT AT CREEKWOOD LAKE AND ADMIRED the calmness of the water. The only sounds he heard were from across the lake, where there looked to be some kind of construction going on. The beginnings of an apartment building, he thought.

A few days had passed since Gus admitted everything to Janice. They still hadn't spoken to each other and he was surprised she was still living at the house with him. It was only a matter of time before she would leave him, he thought.

Gus was suddenly distracted by a silver Mustang pulling up in the distance behind him. He turned and watched the car drive closer to him across the open dirt area. The car came to a stop only a few feet away from him. The door opened, and Becker stepped out. He shut the door and approached Gus.

"Alright, what's so important that I had to come here?" Becker asked.

Gus looked at Becker and paused for a moment. He knew what he had to say, but he didn't know how to begin.

"Kid, I had a long shift last night. I've got a ton of paperwork that needs to get done, and I'm runnin' on almost twenty-four hours of no sleep. Now's not the time to be jerkin' my chain."

"I need to tell you something," Gus said.

"No shit, I kinda figured that out already."

Gus couldn't bring himself to look Becker in the eyes, instead choosing to look off to the side of him.

"It's about...well, you know."

"No, I don't know. The fuck is it?" Becker asked.

"The murder."

Becker started to get irritated.

"Kid, I told you we're past that. We don't ever talk about it again."

Gus finally looked him in the eyes.

"But I need to. You don't understand."

"Oh, I don't? Try me."

"That's not what I meant. There's more to what happened."

"Okay, enlighten me then."

Gus took a deep breath and prepared for whatever reaction Becker would have.

"It wasn't Brian who was messing around with Claudia. It was me." Gus said.

Becker stared at Gus with no expression.

"No shit Sherlock. Do you really think I'm that stupid that I didn't know?"

Gus was taken aback by the words.

"How did you know?"

"That day she came into the station, and you helped her with her car. I saw you acting like a dipshit around her. Not long after, when Art started suspecting something was up, I put two and two together. Plus, I followed you one day. The two of you met up at some motel in Dover Bay."

Gus closed his eyes. He was too embarrassed to keep eye contact with Becker.

"As far as I'm concerned, you're fucking lucky Art didn't find out. And you acting all high and mighty the other night telling me we shoulda turned Art in or taken him down? Yeah, it's on me that kid's dead, but you're the reason all of this happened in the first place. I wouldn't've had to cover your ass if you weren't off porking that bimbo. Don't forget that."

Gus looked down at the ground, the words hitting him hard.

"I know."

"Good. Then do us both a favor and forget all this happened. Move on. What's done is done, and we ain't changing anything."

Becker walked back to his car and opened the door to get in.

"You set that kid up, just to cover for me?" Gus asked.

Becker turned to look at Gus, and his expression changed.

"It's not like it was planned out. The kid walked into Terry's and happened to be in the wrong place at the wrong time. I acted fast and thought I could throw Art off by giving him a potential suspect. When we got to the dunes and I saw how Art was acting, I thought I could pivot and try to get the kid off the hook. I didn't know Art was gonna kill the poor fuck."

Gus didn't know how to react. He was still angry, but also thankful to Becker. Then another thought hit him.

"Do you think Kramer will ever find out what really happened?" Gus asked.

Becker looked at Gus and thought for a moment.

"Maybe. Maybe not. That's the beauty of fate, isn't it?"

Becker got into the car and started it, and Gus watched him as he drove off.

Gus turned back and looked out at the lake, wondering what would happen next.

AUGUST 17, 2023

SEVENTEEN

CHRIS DROVE FAST, BUT NOT TOO FAST. THE LAST THING he needed was a speeding ticket. He drove for what felt like an eternity, his mind racing. Was it true? What Chris had read in that letter seemed impossible. Chris didn't take time to process the letter's contents. He had one goal: to find Larry Becker, the man with all the answers, or so it seemed. But could Chris trust Becker? The mention of Gus to Becker didn't seem to phase him. A police officer with a good poker face, Chris thought.

Chris pulled into the parking lot of Terry's Restaurant, the only place he could think of where he might find Becker. Chris got out of the car and ran inside. The place was mostly empty, with only a few patrons in the dining room. Chris went over to the bar and recognized the bartender from earlier.

"The guy that was here earlier, Becker. Is he still around?"

"No, he left almost an hour ago. Is there something wrong?"

"Do you know where he went or where he could be?"

"My guess is he went home; he was pretty lit when he left here. Plus, there's no other bars in the area."

"Do you have his address?"

The bartender looked at Chris suspiciously and contemplated what his next words were going to be. Chris felt his patience wearing thin.

"Look, I know you barely know me, but it's important that I know where he is. I know he used to be a cop, and I need his help!"

The bartender continued to look at Chris with hesitation.

"I'm not one to beg, but please, this is serious. It's about my father, who passed away recently. He and Becker were close, and I need to ask him some questions."

The bartender sighed, thinking against his better judgment.

"He lives a couple of blocks down on Fillmore Ave. It's the fifth house on the left after you turn onto it, a brown house. I think the house number is 23 or something."

"Thank you."

Chris left a fifty-dollar bill on the countertop and rushed out to his car, speeding out of the lot and down the road until he saw the sign for Fillmore Ave.

He turned left onto the street and immediately saw the brown house on the left-hand side. Chris parked his car a couple of houses away from Becker's, hoping not to raise suspicion. He got out of the car and walked to the front of Becker's house. The sun had set, which would make it harder to see whoever was in the house, Chris thought.

He walked up to the front door and tried to look through the window. Becker's voice startled him.

"You lost or something?"

Chris turned with a jolt, startled to see Becker sitting in a chair in the porch's corner. He had a drink in one hand and a revolver in the other. Chris froze like a deer caught in headlights.

"No, I think I'm right where I need to be."

Chris extended his arms outward, signaling to Becker that he was unarmed. Becker stared at him, not looking the slightest bit phased. Becker motioned towards the front door with the gun.

"Why don't we go inside? It's getting cold out."

Chris tried his best to keep his fear from showing, but inside, he was terrified. Becker got up and motioned for Chris to open the front door. Chris did as he was instructed and walked into Becker's house. Chris stood in the small hallway until Becker was standing next to him. Becker closed the front door, locked it, and then motioned for Chris to walk to the kitchen. Chris walked up to the kitchen table and stood there, waiting for the next instructions. Becker pulled out a chair at the table.

"Have a seat."

Chris sat opposite Becker, who sat at the other end of the table. He kept a hand on the revolver resting on the table. Both men stared at each other while they sat in silence for a moment. Becker smirked.

"Shitting your pants yet, junior?"

Chris said nothing. He stared at Becker, waiting to see what his next move would be. Becker took the revolver off the table and put it in his side holster under his shirt.

"Relax. Jesse from the bar called and said you were coming by. Figured I'd be prepared, plus I wanted to fuck with you a little."

Chris let out a sigh of relief and closed his eyes. Then he regained his composure.

"Why weren't you upfront with me?"

"With what?" Becker asked.

Chris pulled the folded letter from his pocket—the one he read at Gus's house. He tossed it over to Becker. Becker reached over the table for it, unfolding it to look at its contents. He sat there and read it for a minute, his expression as stoic as ever. He put it back on the table.

"Didn't know Gus was a poet."

"Why didn't you tell me any of this?"

"Because it's none of your fucking business."

"The hell it isn't. This is the whole reason he's dead, and you're involved in it!"

"Like fuck I am. I didn't give him the pills; that was his choice."

"So, you did nothing. After everything Kramer did, you, my dad, you both just sat back and did nothing after the fact?"

"If we tried to do anything, we both would've been buried in the ground next to that kid."

"Bullshit, it was two against one; you guys could've taken him down right then and there!"

Becker rubbed his head, getting flashbacks of the similar argument he had with Gus thirty years ago.

"Fuckin' déjà vu," Becker grumbled.

Chris leaned over the table towards Becker.

"Answer me, why didn't you?"

"Kid, your daddy wasn't gonna do anything. He was terrified."

"And you? Were you scared, too?"

Becker sat there stone-faced for a moment. Chris had hoped he struck a nerve with him.

"Yeah, I was. And if you knew Kramer well enough, you would've been too."

It wasn't the response Chris was expecting; it caught him off guard.

"I know I'm responsible for that kid's death. If I hadn't made the call to Kramer that night, he'd still be alive. That's on me. But let's remember, your dad wasn't a saint in all of this."

Chris knew what Becker was referring to.

"Would Kramer have found out what was really going on? Did he even have any idea?" Chris asked.

"Look, I'll give your old man credit. What he did was ballsy and stupid, yes. But he was smart enough to try and cover his tracks. He knew Claudia and Art were an item, but he didn't care. He was stupid enough to ruin his marriage and bang Art's girlfriend. Honestly, I'm shocked that he didn't get caught. I guess that's why I reacted the way I did when Art figured out that Claudia was hooking up with someone behind his back."

"What do you mean you reacted the way you did?"

"Kid, Art's a smart man. He would've picked up on your father, eventually. He was already starting to think that it might be another cop. I tried to throw Art off so he wouldn't suspect your dad. I probably would've done things a little differently had I known Art was gonna blow the kid's head off."

"So, why did you protect my dad?"

"Because cops look out for each other; that's the code. Kramer doesn't believe in it. All he cares about is how to make himself look good. I've realized over the years what a piece of shit he can be, but he's a powerful piece of shit."

Chris took all of this in, not knowing how to react. Becker folded the letter and slid it across the table.

Chris took the letter and put it in his pocket. His shoulders slumped. He looked defeated.

"Look, there's not much else we can do about it. Gus killed himself. That was his choice. It's got nothing to do with us. Everything in that letter died with him, as far as I'm concerned."

"And Kramer?"

"Fuck him. He's not worth going after at this point. He covered his tracks long ago."

"After everything he did, he's just gonna get away with it?" Chris asked.

"He already got away with it; it's been thirty years."

"He's responsible for all of this, though. For my dad..."

"Your dad did what he did. That's not on Kramer. We all had our part in what happened. If your old man had kept his dick in his pants, the whole thing with Claudia wouldn't have happened in the first place."

Though he didn't want to admit it, Chris knew Becker was right. After thinking it through, he realized that this all started with Gus and his actions. From the look on Chris's face, Becker could see that he had struck a nerve, and for the first time, he felt sympathy for him.

"Look, you want some advice? Take the letter and burn it. Scatter your dad's ashes somewhere nice, get the hell out of here, and don't look back."

"What about Claudia?"

"She's the last person you wanna get involved with. The only smart thing she did was take off; you should do the same."

Chris stared blankly at the table, trying to decide his next move. He knew Becker was right; the best thing to do would be to leave.

"You're right," Chris admitted.

"Of course I'm right. Now get the fuck out of my house."

Chris stood up from the table and walked to the front door; Becker followed behind him.

"Take my advice, kid. Get outta here as fast as you can and try to move on from all this shit. It's not worth holding onto," Becker said.

"Yeah. Thanks."

Becker nodded, then shut the door. Chris stood on the porch for a minute, replaying everything in his head, then decided. Tomorrow, he would get Gus's remains and get out of Dayville for good.

— EIGHTEEN

CHRIS DROVE BACK TO GUS'S APARTMENT, DETER-
mined to tie up the last of the loose ends. He would go
through everything, and whatever items he wanted to take,
he would. Tomorrow, he would go to the funeral parlor and
collect Gus's ashes, then escape this town, and never return.

As Chris pulled into the driveway, the eerie stillness of the
empty lot unsettled him once more. It was dark and quiet.
Chris wondered for a moment if anyone even lived in any of
the other apartments in the building. Chris parked the car
and sat there for a moment. He was about to get out when
his phone went off. Chris took out his phone, looked at the
screen, and saw Jessica calling him. He swiped to answer.

"Hey, I'm sorry. I meant to call you earlier, but I got
caught up with a few things."

"No worries, just making sure you haven't forgotten
about me."

"How's everything on your end?"

"Good, just watching a movie and painting my toenails."

"I'll trade places with you, except for the toenail thing."

Chris looked through the windshield at the property, making sure nobody was around. His eyes caught the lake in

front of him, and for a moment, he felt calm. Jessica's voice distracted him.

"Still having fun back home?"

"Yeah, loads. I'll bore you with the details when I get back."

"And when's that gonna be?"

"Tomorrow if all goes well, which it never does, so probably Thursday."

"Well, for what it's worth, I miss you. I hope everything is okay."

"I miss you too. Yeah, just a lot of stuff to process right now; like I said, it's a long story."

Chris looked out of the passenger side window and into the darkness of the woods. Everything still seemed quiet and still.

"I should get going. I'm at the old man's place now. Just gonna wrap up a few things here, then get some sleep."

"Okay. Have fun dreaming about me!"

"I will."

"Nite."

"Goodnight."

Chris looked around the driveway one last time and got out of the car. He walked to the front of the apartment near the door. He was searching his pockets for the keys when he heard a branch snap. Chris turned around but saw nothing. He found the keys and approached the apartment door.

"Evening, Chris," a voice echoed from the darkness behind him.

Chris turned around and saw Art Kramer standing there.

"I hear you've been talking to a few people and asking questions. You working on an article for your paper or something?" Kramer asked.

"Nothing gets by you, huh?"

Chris's heart raced and his adrenaline started kicking in as he caught sight of the handgun clenched in Kramer's left hand. He nodded towards the gun.

"Is that the same gun you used to kill Brian Tate?"

Kramer looked at the gun and smirked.

"Now, why would I do anything like that?" Kramer said as he motioned towards the woods with the gun. "Let's go for a walk. Turn around."

"Fuck you, I'm not going anywhere."

Kramer cocked the hammer back on the gun. The sound sent chills down Chris's spine.

"I'm trying to be a nice guy right now. Please don't make me have to ask twice."

Chris looked towards the woods, then back at Kramer.

"I guess some things never change with you. You're gonna kill me whether it's here or out there, right?"

Kramer stood silent, waiting for Chris to move. Chris relented and turned around. Before he started walking, Kramer stopped him and searched him.

"Don't worry, I'm not armed."

Kramer took Chris's phone from out of his pocket.

"A recording can be just as dangerous."

Kramer dropped the phone to the ground and stomped on it, destroying it. Chris looked down at the phone and shrugged.

"So much for having a screen protector."

"I think that's the least of your worries right now. Let's go," Kramer said.

Chris walked towards the woods with Kramer following behind him.

"I know what you did," Chris said.

"I figured you'd add it all up. You seem like a smart kid.

You take after your old man. How's Becker, by the way, still a drunk?"

"Funny how you seem to know every little thing that goes on around here."

"I have eyes and ears everywhere. When you're a man in my position, you have friends you can rely on."

Chris thought for a few seconds; then it hit him: Jesse, the bartender. He must have been listening to the conversation at the bar with Becker.

"Must be nice," Chris said.

"Keep moving."

They walked deep into the woods. Chris thought they must've walked almost a mile when they approached an open area in the woods. There was nothing in sight. He heard Kramer close behind him.

"This'll do, stop."

Chris followed the instructions. Kramer walked around to face Chris, staring deep into his eyes, and lifted his arm to point the gun at him.

"So now what, you're going to kill me for learning the truth? Even though I never went looking for anything?" Chris asked.

"What can I say? You were in the wrong place at the wrong time."

"Look, whatever happened between you, Becker, and my dad is none of my business; I don't give a shit about any of it anymore. I just wanna settle my dad's affairs and get the hell out of here."

"Kid, believe it or not, I wish I could let you go, but I can't. You're a reporter, and for all I know, you could talk to someone. Then what? We get unwanted attention around here. That's not necessary."

"There isn't more to it?" Chris asked.

Chris wondered if, after all these years, Kramer still didn't know the truth about Claudia and Gus.

"Like I said, you're in the wrong place at the wrong time."

"Or maybe if you weren't such a hothead and didn't blow that guy's brains out, maybe none of this would've happened."

Kramer smirked at the comment, keeping his gun pointed at Chris.

"Are you finished?" Kramer asked.

"Yeah, I guess I am."

Kramer leaned in and put pressure on the trigger when suddenly, he heard leaves crunching in the distance. Kramer turned to look and spotted a deer walking towards the lake nearby.

Chris took advantage of the distraction and did the only thing he could think of now; he ran at Kramer as fast as he could, using all his weight to knock him to the ground. The gun went off as both men hit the ground.

Chris gripped Kramer's left arm with both hands, slamming it into the ground over and over until the gun slipped free. The gun hit the ground, and Chris swiped it away as far as he could. Chris turned and saw Kramer's right hand coming at him, hitting him in the center of his face. The punch dazed Chris, and he stumbled off Kramer. As Chris tried to regain his footing, he saw Kramer run at him. Kramer pinned Chris into a nearby rock and, with his right hand, punched Chris as hard as he could on the side of his head. The blow knocked Chris down to the ground, and he felt dazed once again. As Chris lied on the ground trying to come to his senses, Kramer approached him and reached down to turn Chris over. As Chris felt Kramer's hands on him, he saw a palm-sized rock underneath him.

Chris grabbed the rock without Kramer noticing, and when Kramer turned him over, Chris used the rock and hit

Kramer on the side of his head as hard as he could. Kramer stumbled off Chris and crashed to the ground. Chris looked at Kramer, underestimating his own power for a moment, and stumbled to get to his feet. Kramer was groggy, but he started to move. As he did, Chris ran as fast as he could away from Kramer, who reached down and grabbed the gun that was next to him.

"You little fuck," Kramer grumbled as he fired a shot towards Chris.

Chris jumped behind a tree just before the shot rang out. The bullet hit the wider tree to his left. Chris crouched down to the ground and began crawling as quietly as he could. He looked up and could see Kramer in the distance. Kramer pointed the gun in his direction and fire another shot; this time, the bullet was farther away from Chris. He could tell Kramer was struggling with his aim. Chris stayed close to the ground and didn't move, not wanting any sounds to give Kramer any sign of where he was hiding. Kramer started creeping towards him. Chris could see the blood flowing from the gash on the side of Kramer's head.

Chris resisted the urge to run. He knew Kramer couldn't see him, but the closer Kramer got, the greater the chance he would spot him. Chris saw a nearby rock that was big enough for him to hide behind. He took a chance and ran towards it. As he started running, his foot slipped into a small hole in the ground that was hidden by the leaves. As Chris hit the ground with a thud, he heard a shot fire in his direction. The bullet hit a tree that was only a few feet away from him. Chris limped toward the rock, each step sending jolts of agony through his twisted ankle. When Chris reached the rock, another bullet was fired. This time, it grazed the side of the rock, inches from Chris's head, sending fragments of pebbles into Chris's face.

Chris threw himself to the ground and stayed down, wiping the debris from his face.

He noticed specs of blood on his face from where the pebbles had hit him; luckily, none of them went into his eyes. Chris got to his feet and looked around the corner of the rock; he saw Kramer point the gun at him and fire another shot. Chris ducked just in time for the bullet to miss his head. Kramer was getting closer, and his aim was getting better.

"I can see you, you little bastard. Come out and make this easy for me; I'm an old man, after all."

Another bullet struck the side of the rock, and Chris moved further away from the edge of the rock. Chris looked down and saw a thick tree branch a few feet long. He picked it up; it felt solid enough to use as a weapon. Chris braced himself, waiting for Kramer to get close enough to the side of the rock where Chris could take a swing at him. He then heard a voice call out in the distance.

"Drop the gun, Art."

Chris tried to register what was happening. The voice sounded like Becker's. Chris stuck his head out from behind the rock to see Kramer turn and look to his right. Chris looked further to see Becker walking towards Kramer with his gun drawn. Kramer looked confused for a moment, then kept his hands out to his sides.

"Larry?"

"Don't make me say it again, asshole."

"Well, isn't this the little reunion? You're looking pleasantly unfit; I see the booze is treating you well!"

Becker kept his gun drawn at Kramer, and then he cocked the hammer back.

"Keep talking, motherfucker," Becker said.

"Come on, Larry, you know this needs to happen. He knows too much. Think about what it'll do to us if we let him go. He's gonna go tell his friends, then there's gonna be a shitshow here. There's no reason to revisit the past."

"This shit ends now, Art. It should've ended thirty years ago with you in handcuffs."

"Now, that's not a nice way to talk to someone who saved your life, is it?"

Becker remembered the warehouse, Kramer taking the slug to the chest that was intended for him. Becker shook it off and kept his gun pointed at Kramer.

"Considering what I've done for you since then, I'd say we're even."

"You're making a big mistake, old friend. Get lost and drink away the rest of your retirement. Let me handle this."

Becker fired a shot into the tree inches away from Kramer's head.

"That's my only warning. Drop it," Becker said.

"Could've fooled me. I thought you were just a lousy shot." Kramer said.

Chris was halfway out from behind the rock. He could see Becker's eyes glimpse him briefly.

"Get outta here, junior. We're about to have some fun," Becker said, moving his eyes back to Kramer.

Chris moved out from behind the rock and backed away. In a quick move, Kramer pointed and fired his gun at Chris. The bullet tore into Chris's left shoulder, sending him crashing to the ground as searing pain erupted across his body. As Chris hit the ground, Becker fired a shot at Kramer, the bullet striking him in his left ribcage. The force from the bullet pushed Kramer against a tree behind him. Kramer stood for a moment, looking down at the wound. Then, he looked up at Becker and, with another quick movement, pointed his gun at him. Before Becker could react, Kramer fired a bullet that struck Becker in the upper right side of his chest. Becker fell to the ground and didn't move, as Kramer leaned against the tree, then fell.

Chris laid on the ground, facing up towards the sky. He heard the shots ring out but didn't look to see what had happened. He leaned up, but as he did, there was another moment of intense pain in his shoulder from where the bullet had struck him. Moaning in pain, he tried to keep his voice down and not attract any attention. He laid back down on the ground for a few moments, took a deep breath, and then tried to get back up again.

Reaching out with his right hand, he grabbed onto a tree branch and lifted himself. He slowly walked over to Becker, who was still motionless and lying on the ground. The blood was seeping through his shirt where the gunshot wound was. Chris knelt next to Becker and tried to wake him, but he was motionless. Chris felt weak and fell to his other knee. He started to crawl away, and as he did, he started getting weaker. He then stopped and sat on the ground, trying to remain as calm as he could.

Then, an uneasy feeling came over him. He turned to look up behind him and saw Kramer standing there. He was bleeding from his gunshot wound, but he was able to keep his composure. With a chilling calmness, Kramer raised his gun, aimed it at Chris's face, and pulled the trigger.

NINETEEN

CLICK.

Chris flinched at the sound of the empty chamber. Kramer lifted the gun, examining it for a moment, then lowered it.

"Fuck," Kramer mumbled.

Chris felt a brief wave of relief but was unsure of what to do next. Weak and on the verge of passing out, he watched as Kramer tossed the gun to the ground and leaned over.

"Couldn't make this easy for me, huh?

Chris tried to crawl away with his good arm, but he was too slow and too weak.

"Looks like I'm just going to kill you with my bare hands," Kramer said.

He reached down towards Chris with both hands and gripped his throat. Chris tried to pry Kramer's hands off of him but couldn't. Even in his weakened condition, Kramer still had a strong grip on him. Chris's face started to turn red, his vision becoming blurry.

"Come on, just give in already," Kramer said through clenched teeth.

Suddenly, the top of the tree next to Kramer exploded with a shotgun blast. The sound was deafening, and Kramer quickly released his grip. Both he and Chris looked up. In the distance stood a figure pointing a shotgun at Kramer. Then came a voice.

"Get away from him, now."

Kramer stood upright, raising his hands before him. He backed away from Chris as instructed.

"I think you need to turn around and walk away," Kramer called out.

The person chambered another round and started walking towards Kramer, keeping the shotgun raised at him. Kramer cleared his throat. "This doesn't concern you. I suggest you walk away now."

"I suggest you keep moving away from him if you want to keep your head attached," the person said.

As the figure approached, Chris could make out more details. It was a woman with long, greying hair and a thin frame. He recognized her as she glared at Kramer, waiting for him to make a move. Kramer stared blankly at her for a few moments before he could say anything. Then his expression changed.

"Claudia?"

"Keep moving," Claudia said as she walked closer to where Chris was lying.

Kramer backed up a few more feet, then stopped.

"Claudia, wow! I've gotta say you look great!"

Claudia fired a shot into Kramer's left shoulder, sending him crashing against a tree and writing in pain.

"That's for putting your hands on me, you son of a bitch."

Kramer groaned and tried to steady himself against the tree as Claudia chambered another round and slowly pointed the shotgun at him again. Kramer started breathing heavily but tried to compose himself as he watched her walk closer to him. He smirked at her.

"Still pissed about that little incident, huh?"

Claudia inched closer toward Kramer, glaring at him like a predator stalking its prey.

"Come on, Claudia. You don't wanna do this. This isn't who you are. Just drop the gun, and we can talk."

"Remember the words you said to me, Art?"

Kramer looked at her, the expression of pain on his face changing to confusion.

"You don't remember, do you?" She asked.

Kramer looked down at his wounds, then looked up at her, still confused.

"Sorry, darling. Old age is getting the best of me these days; memory isn't what it used to be." He said sarcastically.

"The last time you looked into my eyes, you told me that if you ever saw me again, you'd kill me," she said, keeping the shotgun pointed at him.

Kramer's expression now turned to panic.

"Do you remember saying those words?"

Kramer stared at her, not knowing what else to say that would change anything.

"Yes, I remember," he said.

She kept the shotgun steadily aimed at Kramer, her finger lightly touching the trigger.

"Look, Claudia, for what it's worth, I didn't mean..."

Claudia fired another round, this one into Kramer's chest. The impact slammed him back against the tree. He grunted as he looked down and saw the blood seeping through the center of his shirt. He looked up at her in shock as he slid to the ground, blood slowly dripping out of his mouth. He fell to the ground and didn't move again.

"That's for Brian."

She approached his body and looked down, then closed her eyes for a moment. She then turned to look back over at Chris, who was still on the ground.

She rushed over to him, lowered the shotgun, and knelt beside him. She placed her hand on his shoulder.

Chris tried to study her face. She looked like she did in the picture he had seen, only older.

"Stay with me," she said.

She took her coat off and slid it under his head. He squinted his eyes as he tried to focus on her, but he was getting weaker.

"Chris?" she called out.

She raised her hand to the side of his face, trying to keep him awake.

"Mom," he whispered, then passed out.

FEBRUARY 7, 1994

➤ TWENTY

THE ROADS WERE EMPTY AS GUS DROVE PAST A SIGN that read "**Pottsville**," a town in western Massachusetts.

Just a couple of hours earlier, he had received a call from Claudia. It had been nearly a year since he had last seen or spoken to her, since that day on his front porch. The day he told Janice everything, the day his life changed because of his involvement in the murder of Brian Tate.

Enough time had passed for Gus to process everything, but he knew his life would never be the same. He would live every day as best he could, with guilt constantly looming over him.

His relationship with Janice had changed. They slept in separate beds and lived practically separate lives. Janice had strong views and didn't believe in divorce, and Gus didn't want to be away from her, either. So, they made things work the best they could, more like roommates than spouses.

Gus looked at the directions he had written earlier when Claudia called. That he was taking this risk behind Janice's back was bad enough. He had no intention of sleeping with Claudia. He vowed to still be faithful to Janice, even though their love life was nonexistent.

Claudia had practically begged to see him over the phone, saying it was important. At first, he refused, but she quickly

reminded him of his promise—that if she ever needed anything, he would help her in any way he could.

He continued driving, mentally preparing himself for
whatever might happen when he saw Claudia. He took the
exit off the highway, made a right turn, and drove for another
fifteen minutes.

The area was becoming more rural by the minute. Soon,
there was nothing but trees and the occasional house. Finally,
he saw the street sign for "Highland Ave." Gus made a left
turn onto a dirt road and drove until he found the house
marked by the number 76 on the mailbox at the beginning
of the driveway. He turned right and slowly drove down the
driveway until he reached its end. The house was a two-story
ranch. It looked as though it had been built within the last
few years. Gus looked around before getting out of the car.

A young Australian Cattle Dog ran up to him, barking
energetically. Gus extended his hand, allowing the dog to
sniff it. The dog licked Gus's hand before darting towards
the house and barking a few more times. Gus glanced at the
wraparound front porch and saw Claudia standing at the
edge of the steps. She hadn't changed a bit, except maybe her
hair was a little longer than Gus remembered.

He walked over to the porch and stopped at the bottom
of the steps. Claudia smiled at him.

"Hey, stranger."

"Hey to you," Gus replied.

He couldn't help but stare into her eyes, but he kept his
emotions in check. Things were different now, and he wanted
to keep it that way.

"Nice place. I'm glad things are going well for you."

"Thanks. It took a little while, but I'm happy."

They continued to gaze at each other for a few more
moments.

"So, what was so important that I had to drive out here?"

"Do you want to come inside so we can talk?"

Gus hesitated before answering.

"Claudia, things are different now. I just want you to know that."

"I know. It's not like that, trust me."

"Okay," he said.

Gus walked up the steps and onto the porch, following Claudia to the front door and into the house. The kitchen was spacious and had a rustic charm, with an island in the center and pots and pans hanging from the ceiling. Claudia went over to the counter, opened an overhead cabinet, and retrieved two glasses.

"Can I get you some water or anything?"

"Water is fine, thanks."

Gus walked over to the island as Claudia filled both glasses with water and brought them over. She took a seat on a chair at one end and gestured for Gus to sit at the other. He sat down across from her and took a sip from his glass.

"How are things back home?" she asked.

"Good, nothing much has changed."

"How's the job going?"

"It's tolerable for the moment."

"How are you doing with everything?"

He knew what she was referring to. He had hoped the subject of the murder wouldn't come up, but deep down, he knew it would eventually.

"Okay. I try not to think about it much."

"And Art?"

"He carried on like nothing ever happened."

Claudia went silent for a moment, taking a few sips of her water.

"Have you heard from him?" he asked.

"No," she said, shaking her head. "And if I ever see him again, I'll kill him myself."

Her words surprised Gus. He had never known Claudia to be a violent person. Something changed in her the day Kramer attacked her. Gus wanted to ask more questions about it but figured it would be best to drop the subject.

"I'm sorry. I didn't mean to bring it up."

"Don't worry about it. It only made me realize how much stronger I can be. His time will come."

Gus heard a banging noise coming from upstairs. Instinctively, he quickly stood up and placed his hand on the handle of his service revolver, which was strapped to his side. He always carried it, even when he was off duty.

Claudia quickly raised her hand to pause him.

"It's okay, hold on a second."

She walked out of the kitchen, through the living room, and up a set of stairs around the corner. Gus remained still, taking his hand off the revolver but staying ready in case something went wrong. Upstairs, he heard more noise, but it sounded muffled. He continued to wait cautiously. A minute later, Claudia came back downstairs and returned to the table.

"Sorry," she said

"Everything okay?"

"Yeah, just..."

Another banging noise came from upstairs.

"Dammit. Sorry, I'll be right back," she said, getting up and heading towards the stairs again.

"Anything I can help with?"

Claudia paused for a moment to think it over.

"I don't know."

Gus stood up and walked over to meet Claudia at the bottom of the stairs.

"What can I do?" he asked.

She nodded to him to follow her up the stairs. He followed her to the top and down a short hallway, then she stopped at the bedroom door. She gestured for Gus to go in.

Gus walked into the room first and, at once, noticed a crib in the corner. Various images of children's cartoons decorated the room. He glanced back at Claudia, who stood behind him. She nodded, encouraging him to approach the crib. Gus turned and walked over to it. Looking down, he saw a baby with big brown eyes and a small patch of light brown hair staring up at him. Gus gazed at the baby for a moment, then turned to look at Claudia, who was smiling.

"When did this happen?" he asked.

"I had him a few months ago."

Gus turned back to look at the baby again, genuinely happy for her. He continued to stare into the baby's eyes, and then a thought struck him. He turned back to look at Claudia, who was watching him, a tear rolling down her cheek.

"That means you were pregnant when we last saw each other?"

"Yes," she nodded, trying to hold back more tears.

Gus stared at her blankly, his mind racing. He looked back down into the crib and looked into the baby's eyes, then studied his facial features. He looked back at Claudia.

"Is he...?"

"Yes," Claudia said as her bottom lip quivered.

Gus felt as though the ground was shifting beneath him. He placed a hand on the edge of the crib to steady himself. Claudia moved toward him, but he raised his other hand to stop her.

"Gus, I'm so sorry. When I went to your house that day, that's what I was going to tell you. I had just found out, and I wanted to tell you before I left so that we could try to figure things out. But then you told me Janice was pregnant, and I couldn't say anything after that. Ever since then, I've been trying to find the right way to tell you without making things worse between you two."

Gus continued to stand in silence, struggling to find the right words.

"Janice had a miscarriage. Not long after I last saw you."

Claudia put her hands to her mouth, feeling a wave of guilt wash over her.

"Gus...."

Gus straightened up and looked back down into the crib. "Things happen."

They both stood there, staring down at the baby. Claudia slowly moved closer, standing beside Gus and placing a hand on his shoulder. She could see a tear forming in his eye.

"His name is Christopher. I named him after my father. I hope that's okay."

Gus nodded his head in approval.

"Yes. It's a good name."

They both continued to stare into the crib for what seemed like forever. Gus felt overwhelmed with different emotions.

"Do you want to hold him?"

Gus looked at her cautiously.

"Is it okay?"

"Of course!"

Claudia reached into the crib and picked up Chris. He made a few noises as she held him for a moment, then she handed him over to Gus, who held him as if he were the most fragile thing on earth.

Claudia gently adjusted Gus's hands to help him hold the baby properly. Gus held Chris close to his chest, feeling the baby's gentle breathing. He looked at Claudia, his face filled with shock.

"I don't know what I'm supposed to do."

"You'll figure it out quickly. It's all instinct."

Gus continued to hold Chris for a while until he finally fell asleep in his arms. Claudia helped Gus place Chris back in the crib and tuck him in. They both went back downstairs and stood in the living room. Gus looked out the bay window that overlooked the woods in the backyard.

"Gus, I want you to take him."

The words hit Gus like a brick. He felt shocked by the words he had just heard.

"You what?!"

Claudia raised her hand to signal Gus to let her finish.

"He won't be okay with me. There are a lot of things going on that I can't get into right now. I'm going to be leaving in a month, and I don't know how long I'll be gone for."

Gus was still in a state of shock and confusion.

"I don't understand. Why can't you tell me—"

"You don't need to know," Claudia interrupted. "He'll be safer with you and Janice."

Gus tried to remain calm and make sense of everything he was hearing.

"Claudia, this is too much, too fast. How am I going to have enough time to tell Janice about this and get her on board with the whole idea?"

"There has to be a way to figure it out, Gus. Christopher isn't safe with me."

"Claudia, what the hell is going on? Are you in trouble or something? Is it Art?"

"It's not him. You just have to trust me on this."

"How can I trust you if you're not being upfront with me about everything?"

"Gus, please."

"This isn't fair, Claudia. You can't just dump this on me suddenly and run away. We need time to figure this out!"

"Time isn't on my side right now, Gus. You have to take Christopher, and it needs to happen soon."

"What's going on? Talk to me!"

"I'm not capable of taking care of him."

"What do you mean? Look around you; you've done a great job with him!"

"Ever since that day when Art confronted me, I haven't been the same. I'm always on edge, and I feel like I'm going to snap and do something horrible. I need to get away from everything. Please, I just need you to take him for a while. For his safety and mine. Please, Gus," she said, reaching across the table to hold his hand.

Gus looked down and gently pulled his hand away.

"I need time to figure this out with Janice. Please, I can't just spring this on her and expect her to go along with it right away."

Claudia withdrew her hands and sat quietly.

"Just a little bit of time, Claud, that's all I'm asking."

"Fine."

Gus stood up and finished his glass of water.

"I should go. I'm going to tell Janice all this tonight. Give it a few days to cool off, and I'll call you. Then we can figure out the next step."

"Okay."

Gus looked into her eyes for a moment, then turned to leave. He heard Claudia's voice behind him.

"You don't want him, do you?"

Gus turned to face her, but he couldn't look her in the eyes.

"He reminds you of what we had, and you want to forget about that and act like everything between us never happened. That's it, isn't it?"

Gus stood at the door, silent. She was right—this wasn't something he wanted. It wouldn't be fair to Janice. He desperately wanted to move on from the mess he had created. But he couldn't say that to Claudia. She seemed so fragile now that telling her how he felt would crush her.

"Give me a few days. We'll figure this out, I promise."

Claudia nodded as she watched Gus leave the house. She stood up and walked over to the front door, watching as Gus stopped to pet the dog.

A thought then occurred to him. He didn't want to ask Claudia the question, but he felt he had to in order to put his mind at ease. He turned back to her.

"Are you sure he's mine?"

She nodded her head.

"You're certain he's not Art's?"

"He can't have kids," she said.

He nodded, then turned and got into his car. He looked in the rearview mirror at Claudia, who was still standing on the porch.

He pulled out of the driveway, and her eyes stayed on his car until he drove off into the distance.

TWENTY-ONE

A FEW DAYS PASSED AFTER GUS TOLD JANICE ABOUT the child he had with Claudia. For Janice, it felt like someone had torn open an old wound all over again. She wanted to leave Gus, never to see him again, but a small part of her wouldn't let go; he was her husband, after all.

Even through all the pain that he caused her, there was a part of her that still loved him. But that love was fading, little by little. She decided to wait until there was nothing left to feel for him.

IT WAS EARLY in the afternoon when Gus finished mowing the lawn. He walked into the house and saw Janice sitting at the kitchen table. It had become a habit for Janice to leave the room whenever Gus entered, so she got up from the table, took her plate of crackers and cheese, and went into the living room.

She never so much as looked at him, and Gus was used to it by now. He went over to the sink to get a glass of water. When he was done, he walked down the hall towards the bathroom to take a shower. He had just turned the faucet on when he heard Janice's voice from the living room.

"GUS!"

Instinctively, Gus got his revolver and ran out of the bathroom, down the hall, and into the living room. He froze as he saw Janice standing in the doorway, looking down at the ground.

The door was open, and there was a stroller in front of her. As soon as Gus saw the stroller, he instantly knew that it had to be Christopher. Claudia had left him at their doorstep. Gus rushed next to Janice, and they both looked at Christopher lying in the stroller.

"I heard a noise at the door," Janice said.

Gus continued to stare at the stroller in shock.

"Gus, what the hell is going on? "

Gus moved past Janice, looked outside, then backc at her.

"Stay in the house and close the door."

"What about the baby?"

"NOW!"

Janice shut the door, and Gus ran to the front of the yard, his gun still drawn. He checked both sides of the yard but found nothing. He went back to the front of the house and looked back down at the stroller.

"Dammit, Claud, why did you do this?"

He opened the front door and pushed the stroller into the house, then closed the door and locked it behind him. He walked past Janice, through the kitchen, and out the back door.

Gus checked the backyard first, then he checked the shed, but he found nothing. He went back into the house and locked the door. He walked into the living room, where Janice stood next to the stroller.

"Is that him, Gus?"

"Yes."

"She just left him?"

"I couldn't find her outside."

"So, he could've been out there for hours!"

"Please calm down; let's try to figure this out…"

"She left her child on our doorstep, Gus. What are you going to figure out?"

"Claudia has no family. I can contact child services and report this."

"And then what?"

"They'll take him and probably place him in some kind of care if they can't find Claudia. He'll be okay."

Janice glared at Gus. She finally reached her breaking point.

"Damn you and that whore."

Gus moved closer to her.

"What did you just…"

"You heard me, you son of a bitch!" Janice yelled out.

Gus stopped and was silent. He had never seen Janice so angry before. She was like a different person.

"I won't let you or her ruin this child's life by putting him in some foster home with strangers."

"What do you think we are?"

"You're his father, you asshole! And if you won't be a parent to this child, then I will."

Gus stood there in shock, not knowing what else to say. Janice inched closer to him. He braced himself in case she tried to hit him.

"I'll take care of him, and so will you, until she shows her face again—if she ever does."

"Janice, we can't do this."

"Yes, we can, and we're going to."

"Janice…"

"If this child goes, then I go. And if I go, I promise you

these last few months will seem like a vacation compared to what I'll do to you."

Gus didn't have the energy to argue with her anymore. He knew the decision had been made, and he no longer had the energy to argue with her.

"You don't know what you're doing." Gus said. "We'll figure it out; and for once in your life, you're going to man up and do the right thing."

He slowly walked past her and to the kitchen, where he stood by the window, and stared out into the backyard.

AUGUST 18, 2023

TWENTY-TWO

CHRIS'S EYES SLOWLY OPENED TO A BLURRY WHITE surface that gradually came into focus—a white ceiling. He lifted his head slightly off the pillow, realizing he was in a hospital room.

He noticed the IV drip and the sticky patches on his skin connected to a heart monitor. The pain in his shoulder wasn't as intense as before, but he still felt the burning sensation from where the bullet hit him. He looked around the rest of the room without moving his head, which seemed like a private room since there were no other patients in the room with him.

"About time you woke up," a familiar voice called out.

Chris turned and saw Jessica sitting down next to his bed. She stood up and moved closer to him, taking his hand. He smiled at her.

"You enjoy the drive here?"

"Never mind that. How are you feeling?"

"Like I got hit by a train."

He could feel her holding his hand tighter. He looked down at her hand, then back up at her.

"How did you know I was here?"

"You told the hospital to contact me."

Chris's mind still felt foggy. He was struggling to remember how he ended up here.

"I don't remember any of it."

"I know. They told me you were barely conscious when they brought you in. When they asked you if there was anybody to contact, you gave them my information."

Chris leaned back, trying to remember, but his mind was blank.

"I'm sorry you got involved in this."

"Well, I'm not sure what 'this' is, but you can tell me all about it when you get better. I'm just glad you're okay."

Chris was still struggling to make sense of it all.

"Did anyone mention to you how I got here?"

"They said someone dropped you off, and she wanted to remain anonymous when they tried to get her info."

"Claudia."

"Who?"

"Never mind, it's a long story."

"Is she someone I should worry about? Do I need to cut a bitch?"

Chris tried not to laugh at the comment.

"No," he said.

"We've got a long car ride home when you get out, so you can tell me everything then."

"Deal."

Just then, a nurse walked into the room. She was older, dressed in light blue scrubs. She was reading notes on a tablet.

"Finally awake, I see," she said as she walked over to the bed and looked at the monitor that was hooked up to him. "How are we feeling?"

"Not bad, considering," Chris said.

The nurse replaced the empty IV bag with a new one.

"And the shoulder, on a scale of one to ten, how is the pain?"

"Probably a six."

"Okay, I'd say that's pretty normal."

Jessica stood up to face the nurse.

"When do you think he'll be ready to go home?"

"If all goes well, I'd say probably tomorrow. We want to keep him under observation for at least another night."

"Wonderful," Chris said as he closed his eyes.

"Could've been a lot worse, my friend. You're very lucky," the nurse said.

Chris knew she was right. Slowly, the events of the last twenty-four hours started to come back to him.

"I'll be back to check on you in a little. Lunch is being served soon," the nurse said as she walked out of the room.

"Thanks," Chris mumbled.

"Is there anything you need me to do while you're in here?" Jessica asked.

"Nothing that I can think of unless you want to swing by the funeral parlor and pick up my father's ashes."

"You can't be serious."

"Okay, how about a coffee from Dunkin' Donuts?"

"Okay, looks like the drugs are kicking in. I'm going to head out for a little and explore. Get some rest. I'll be back later." She leaned in and kissed him on the forehead.

"Sounds good."

He watched Jessica leave, and then he dozed off.

———————

CHRIS WOKE UP a couple of hours later, expecting to see Jessica by his bedside. She wasn't there. Instead, it was Claudia. Chris straightened up in his bed, ignoring the pain but alarmed by her presence. Claudia put her hands up.

"It's okay."

"Like hell it is!"

The heart rate machine hooked up to Chris was beeping faster. Claudia put her hand on Chris's.

"I'm not going to hurt you."

Chris pulled his hand away quickly.

"Who the hell are you, anyway?"

"I think you already know the answer to that. How did you find out, by the way?"

Chris did not want to say anything to her out of spite, but he thought she might already know more than he did.

"He left me a letter telling me a lot more than I wanted to know."

Claudia looked away.

"That makes sense. It sounds like something he would do. He was always looking for a way to confess everything."

"So why the hell are you here? According to the letter, you ditched me and left me on their doorstep. What made you come back after all this time? Guilt?"

"I could do with a little less attitude."

"How did you know where to find me out in the woods?"

"I understand your frustration, but please try to calm down. Now's not the time or place for this."

"No! You tell me everything right now. I'm not waiting. You at least owe me that."

"I saved your life; I don't owe you anything."

"You left me and never came back. I'd say you do!"

Claudia leaned back in the chair. She knew Chris had a point.

"I thought about reaching out to your father. It wasn't until about a year ago. I thought that enough time had passed, so I looked him up, took a chance, and showed up at his place. He told me you had moved and that you and him weren't really talking that much."

"I bet that was quite the reunion," Chris said, his voice cold.

"Did you know he had Alzheimer's?"

Chris looked at her, and his brief expression was enough of an answer for her.

"I guess not. Maybe if you had cared enough, you could've reached out to him. You could've been there for him instead of me," she said.

"Get off your high horse, lady. If you two hadn't hooked up, then maybe none of that mess would've ever happened."

"And you wouldn't even exist."

Chris looked away from her. He couldn't think of anything to argue with that.

"I stayed in the apartment above his so I could be there for him. He was diagnosed a while back but lately it was starting to get worse." she said.

"Well, he had my number; he could've reached out to me."

"And you had his. I'd say you both were in the wrong."

"Well, if he had Alzheimer's, how was he able to remember everything in that letter? Did you help him write it or something?"

"No. Maybe he wrote it and held on to it for a while, who knows."

"He died from an overdose; did you help him with that?"

"No, I went to check on him in the morning and found him." she said, trying to hold back tears.

Chris rested his head back on the pillow, thinking of everything that was written in the letter. He memorized everything in it.

"He told me everything in that letter. The pain he went through, how he regretted everything. What Kramer did to you. How he felt betrayed by Becker. Wait, where's Becker? He was there in the woods with me!"

"He's gone, and good riddance."

Chris went silent. He knew Becker had his demons, but Becker tried to save him. And deep down, Chris thought Becker had regrets of his own and, in his own way, thought he was doing the right thing.

"And Kramer?" Chris asked.

"Gone."

"How did you know where we were?"

"I came back to the apartment and heard the gunshots in the woods, so I went to check it out."

"What about their bodies?"

"I handled everything, and I trust you won't say anything to anyone?"

She looked at Chris with caution.

"At this point, I don't wanna remember anything about this place. I don't want any connection to it. Your secret is safe."

Claudia let out a breath of relief and gave him a small yet genuine smile.

"Look, if you think this is gonna be some kind of bonding moment between us, then you're wrong. Thank you for saving my life. I'll always be grateful to you for that. But if you're looking for anything else from me, then let me make one thing clear: you may be my biological mother, but Janice Collins will always be my mother."

The words hit Claudia hard, but deep down, she understood. She nodded her head.

"I get it. I'll leave you alone then."

Claudia stood and walked to the doorway, looking back at Chris.

"Take care of yourself."

"You too," Chris said as he watched her leave.

← EPILOGUE

CHRIS WALKED ONTO THE DOCK BEHIND GUS'S APART-
ment building, which led out to Creekwood Lake. Chris
walked to the end of the dock and looked out at the water.
This had been Gus's favorite spot to reflect, Chris could now
understand why.

Chris held the urn tightly in both hands, his arm still in a
sling from the wound. Jessica watched from a little further
away on the dock. She offered to go out there with Chris, but
he insisted she stay back.

He wanted one last moment alone with Gus. Chris knelt
at the edge of the dock, placed the urn down, and dipped his
hand into the cool water. He looked over at the rowboat and,
for a moment, thought about untying it and going out to the
center of the lake to scatter the ashes. But with just one good
arm, he decided against it. He removed the lid and looked
inside at the clear bag holding Gus Collins's remains.

"I don't know what to say to you, considering everything
I've found out. You were a complicated person, that's for
sure. But I always loved you. You made it so difficult, though;
you were so distant and always made me feel like I was never
important in your life. There's a lot I wish I could still ask
you, but I can understand some of it now and what could've

happened, and I guess that gives me some answers. But I don't know if I can ever forgive you for the things that you did."

Chris reached into the urn and pulled out the bag. He unrolled the top of it.

"This was always your favorite place, so I'm guessing it'll be okay for you."

Chris took the bag, leaned over the dock above the water, and slowly scattered the remains into the lake. Once the bag was empty, Chris rolled it up and placed it back into the urn. He grabbed the urn, stood up, and looked out into the lake one last time, knowing he would never come back here again. He had no desire to.

"I Love you, Dad."

Chris walked back to where Jessica stood. She walked towards him.

"You okay?" she asked.

"Yeah, I'm good."

They held hands as they walked back to the car, with Chris settling into the passenger seat and Jessica taking the wheel.

"Can I trust your driving for the next four hours?"

Jessica smiled at him and started the car. They drove out of the driveway and onto the main road.

———

AT THE APARTMENT on the top floor, Claudia watched as they drove away. She waited until they were out of sight, then went into the kitchen. She walked over to the table and picked up a folded piece of paper. It was the letter that Gus wrote. She looked it over, then brought it to the counter and dropped it into the kitchen sink. She lit a match and placed it on top of the letter, letting it burn until there was nothing but ashes left.

"No more secrets."

She grabbed her coat and the keys to her black Toyota Camry, walked out of the apartment, and shut the door behind her.

— ACKNOWLEDGMENTS

THIS BOOK WOULD NOT BE POSSIBLE WITHOUT THE help and support of many people. I'd like to thank the following: Maria Cambio for constantly being there and showing me what a better person I can be every day, I love you. To Aria, hopefully when you're old enough Mom will let you read the book. To my family, Robin Heaton, Al Grundy, Deb Heaton, Bill Heaton, Sharon Cambio, and John Cambio, thank you for always being there for me and for showing me that anything can be achieved with hard work and determination, I love you all. A special thank you to Dawn and Steven Porter for allowing me the opportunity to publish my very first novel, and to the team at Stillwater River Publications for their help and support with the whole process. And to you, the reader, thank you for reading the book, I hope you enjoyed it!

Bill Heaton grew up with a deep-rooted passion for storytelling that he brings to life in his debut novel, *Dayville*. When he isn't writing, Bill enjoys exploring the natural beauty of New England through hiking and capturing moments behind the lens of his camera. Bill currently lives in Coventry, Rhode Island, with his family. For more information about Bill and his other books visit **www.billheaton.com**.

Made in the USA
Middletown, DE
23 February 2025